DURARARA!!

DRrr!!

7

D1253444

PALM BEACH COUNTY
LIBRARY SYSTEM
3650 Summit Boulevard
West Palm Beach, FL 33406-4198

RYOHGO NARITA
ILLUSTRATION BY
SUZUHITO YASUDA

"Celty, I love… *Mwuh?*"

His eyes opened.

"…Oh. It was a dream."

Disappointed, Shinra realized that he'd fallen asleep at his desk, and the dancing was all in his head. He stretched and yawned.

But just then, the partner he'd been dancing with in his dreams appeared in the doorway to the bedroom, wearing black pajamas.

"*Morning. You're already awake?*" she typed into her PDA. Shinra gave her an enormous smile, completely banishing any disappointment he might have felt about the letdown.

"Hey! I just woke up myself. An act of true synchronicity! My waking was of the most pleasant type."

"*I see… I had a weird dream. You and I were dancing all through it.*"

"?!"

Shinra's eyes went wide when he saw the text.

Is this true synchronicity?!

"It's a miracle of love, Celty! Quick, let us continue the dream…"

Enraptured, Shinra moved closer to celebrate their synchronization and pick up the bliss of the dream where they had left off—until he saw the next part of her message.

"*We were doing the pond loach dance.*"

"…Y-you mean…like that basket-scooping dance people do when they get really drunk…?"

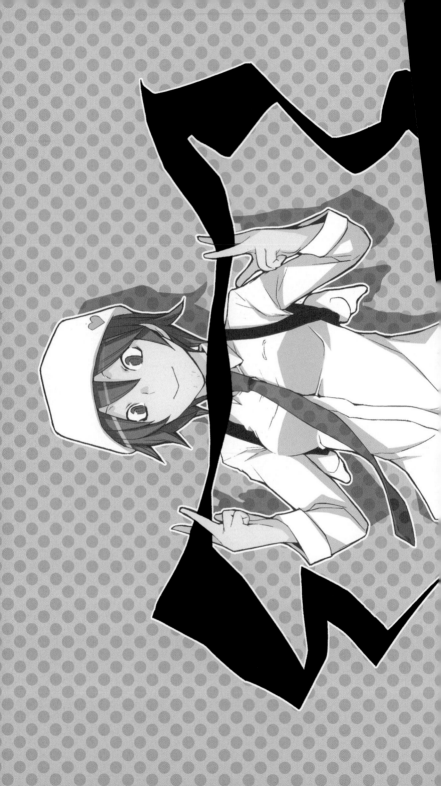

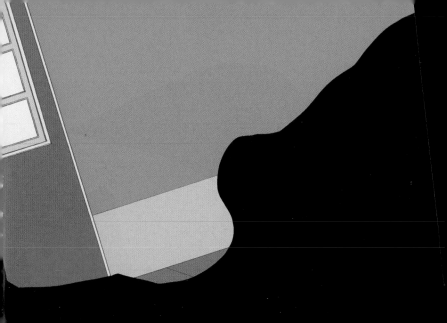

Two shadows bobbed and swayed in the dance hall.

One totally white, one utterly black.

"Celty…you're so beautiful," said the white figure to the woman who wore a black dress fashioned from shadow itself.

"Thank you, Shinra. I love you," came a beautiful voice from the neck of the headless woman.

"Huh? Is that the first time I ever heard your voice, Celty?! Well, I guess that doesn't matter now! Let's dance!"

Shinra grabbed her hand and began to move, unconcerned. A waltz tune started playing in the dance hall, and the two figures dazzled the space with their smooth movements.

"Oh…oh, Celty. I could keep dancing like this for eternity, as long as it means holding hands with you."

"Me too, Shinra."

Celty's entire body pulled inward with shyness. Seeing this, Shinra smoothly pulled her close and squeezed her tight.

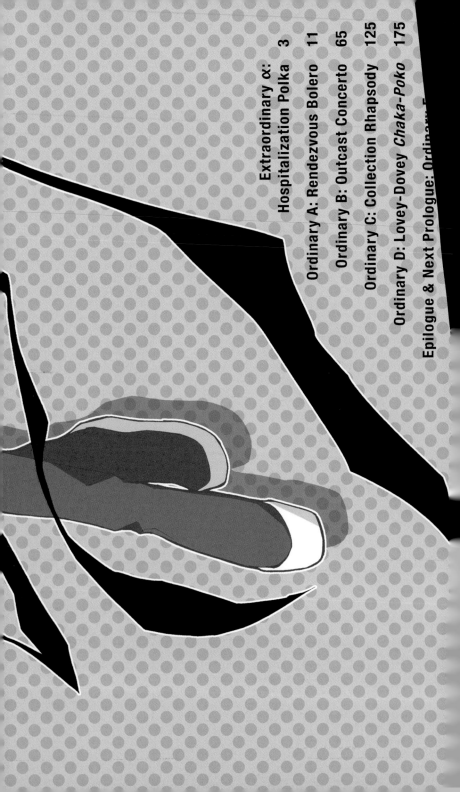

VOLUME 7

Ryohgo Narita
ILLUSTRATION BY **Suzuhito Yasuda**

NEW YORK

DURARARA!!, Volume 7
RYOHGO NARITA
ILLUSTRATION BY SUZUHITO YASUDA

Translation by Stephen Paul
Cover art by Suzuhito Yasuda

This book is a work of fiction. Names, characters, places, and incidents are the product of the author's imagination or are used fictitiously. Any resemblance to actual events, locales, or persons, living or dead, is coincidental.

DURARARA!!
© RYOHGO NARITA 2010
All rights reserved.
Edited by ASCII MEDIA WORKS
First published in 2010 by KADOKAWA CORPORATION, Tokyo.
English translation rights arranged with KADOKAWA CORPORATION, Tokyo,
through Tuttle-Mori Agency, Inc., Tokyo.

English translation © 2017 by Yen Press, LLC

Yen On
1290 Avenue of the Americas
New York, NY 10104

Visit us at yenpress.com
facebook.com/yenpress
twitter.com/yenpress
yenpress.tumblr.com
instagram.com/yenpress

First Yen On Edition: July 2017

Yen On is an imprint of Yen Press, LLC.
The Yen On name and logo are trademarks of Yen Press, LLC.

The publisher is not responsible for websites (or their content) that are not owned by the publisher.

Library of Congress Cataloging-in-Publication Data
Names: Narita, Ryōgo, 1980– author. | Yasuda, Suzuhito, illustrator. | Paul, Stephen (Translator), translator.
Title: Durarara!! / Ryohgo Narita, Suzuhito Yasuda, translation by Stephen Paul.
Description: New York, NY : Yen ON, 2015–
Identifiers: LCCN 2015041320 | ISBN 9780316304740 (v. 1 : pbk.) | ISBN 9780316304764 (v. 2 : pbk.) | ISBN 9780316304771 (v. 3 : pbk.) | ISBN 9780316304788 (v. 4 : pbk.) | ISBN 9780316304795 (v. 5 : pbk.) | ISBN 9780316304818 (v. 6 : pbk.) | ISBN 9780316439688 (v. 7 : pbk.)
Subjects: | CYAC: Tokyo (Japan)—Fiction. | BISAC: FICTION / Science Fiction / Adventure.
Classification: LCC PZ7.1.N37 Du 2015 | DDC [Fic]—dc23
LC record available at http://lccn.loc.gov/2015041320

ISBNs: 978-0-316-43968-8 (paperback)
         978-0-316-47428-3 (ebook)

1 3 5 7 9 10 8 6 4 2

LSC-C

Printed in the United States of America

I've written about the city's holidays in a number of books before this. Today, I'm going to change tacks and talk about human holidays.

A day of rest for a person is meant in a literal sense: to rest one's body.

But in practice, it doesn't work out that way.

During a holiday, people actually go out of their way to travel, to celebrate to the point of exhaustion, to throw themselves into their interests or otherwise expend their physical stamina.

Do you have personal experience with this?

You do, don't you?

You don't?

Fine. I lose.

I apologize.

I'm sorry.

I was ignorant of people.

I made assumptions about people.

Forgive me…! Forgive me!

……I suppose that's enough apologizing for now. I'll now continue speaking to those of you who answered my question in the affirmative.

It's possible that those who use their holidays to tire themselves out are the ones who seek the extraordinary. While it might break from the dictionary definition of the word, a temporary break from the everyday schedule could be considered a form of "rest" for this type of person.

It's not resting the body.

It's not resting the mind.

It's not the body or the mind that relaxes…but the entire "state" of everyday repetition.

By doing this, one is able to enjoy the flavor of ordinary life when it returns.

You know how it works.

It's like taking a sip of water to cleanse the palate when eating good food.

So what do those who lead extraordinary lives do for their day off?

Do urban legends such as the Black Rider even have holidays?

It's tough to answer.

Does someone who always eats extremely rich food take a holiday by drinking water, or do they chug even richer soy sauce instead? That was an example—don't try that at home, or you'll regret it.

You'll…you know…die.

Perhaps those who truly submerge themselves in the extraordinary simply surpass that level and have a certain kind of death wish instead.

Do those folks actually have holidays, or is every day a holiday for them?

We can only learn the truth by asking them.

But the city itself does not differentiate between their ordinary or extraordinary lives, between work and holidays.

Ultimately, it's human beings who view these things and judge them.

The city does not differentiate between its humans. It simply envelops all our actions.

If only it knew that, like soy sauce, it's dangerous to drink too much.

But I suppose that a city's stomach is much stronger than a person would imagine.

> —Excerpt from the preface of Shinichi Tsukumoya, author of
> Media Wax's Ikebukuro travel guide, *Ikebukuro Strikes Back 3*

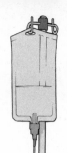

Extraordinary α Hospitalization Polka

DRRR×7

Ryohgo Narita

May 5, Tohoku region, hospital

"It's time for your inspection, Mr. Orihara!" said the young nurse.

The pale hospital room smelled of a mix of chemicals and just a bit of something sweet—either flowers or fruit.

Given that this was a private room, the smell had to be from a gift to whatever patient was next door.

It was with that suspicion in mind that Izaya Orihara's mind rose into wakefulness.

Oh, right. I'm in a hospital, he realized, looking at the unfamiliar woman in the room with him.

"What time is it, ma'am?"

"Let's see—it's nearly nine o'clock at night. Hang on, I'll switch your drip feed."

She promptly rolled back the blanket and the sleeve of his gown, checked the status of the needle in his arm, and then switched out the bag of liquid.

Suddenly, Izaya was aware of a strong pain in his stomach. He squinted, holding his breath against the sensation.

Finally, his wits were sharp again.

He recalled exactly what had happened to put him in this situation.

It had happened twenty-four hours earlier. Someone had stabbed him, and he'd collapsed on the street in a city in northern Japan. And now here he was, waking up in a hospital bed.

It was his third inspection. Or possibly the fourth.

The police had come before dawn, he recalled. Izaya remembered talking to the detectives, as he watched the nurse go about her business.

The detectives had asked him all sorts of questions, but he firmly maintained that something had bumped into him, hard, and then his stomach was bleeding. They asked him for more personal details, but the first greeting they'd given him was "Mr. Orihara," so he knew they were probably at least aware of his address already, among other things.

What started as a solitary journey for enjoyment had ended with a stabbing at the hands of some lunatic, he told the detectives.

"Please, officers, find whoever did this. If not for my sake, then for the peace of mind of the local residents," he pleaded with a smile, though even he had to admit that the act was a bit much.

Izaya Orihara knew that his attacker was not just "some guy," but a man named Jinnai Yodogiri. The man had told him as much on the phone, right before the attack.

But Izaya didn't tell the detectives that.

He wanted to avoid revealing their connection and making things any bigger than they already were. Plus, he knew the police were unlikely to actually catch the man.

He could have made up some kind of description to tell the police, but Izaya didn't know if the shopping area had security cameras and where they might have been or if there were witnesses to the attack—any of which could expose holes in his story.

Any careless lie at this point could come back to bite him, if it were proven false.

Could be too late for that. Izaya smirked to himself, recalling the way the officers had looked at him. *Those weren't gazes of sympathy for an attack victim. They were the searching gazes of hunters. I should assume that they already spotted the knife I keep in the hidden pocket of my coat.*

The police didn't mention it at all, but if they wanted to, they could haul him in for possession of a weapon. He was the victim in this case, but to the local police, he was also a suspicious outsider who might be up to no good.

I should get out of here overnight.

On the very first inspection, he heard about the condition of his wounds. Miraculously, there was hardly any damage to his interior organs. He had no way of knowing whether that had been Yodogiri's intention or not.

Great, guess I'll have to owe Shinra a favor again, he thought, snorting as he envisioned the face of his friend, a black market doctor. *And you can never be certain what he'll do, either...*

Just then, the nurse finished up her task. "You're all done. And looking pretty healthy, if you ask me, so it might not be too long before you're discharged," she said with a grin.

He returned it out of habit. "That's too bad. I was just thinking that this hospital is so comfortable, I wouldn't mind staying longer."

"Are you imagining that flattery will get you something? Listen, you're a young man, but even still, this is quite a healthy recovery. You're practically ready to walk out the day after you got stabbed."

"All thanks to the doctors and nurses here," Izaya said. He wore a smile, but underneath it, darkness lurked.

Yes, the pain was a part of that, but more pressing was the image of a certain man's face, which the nurse's words had put into his head.

The thing is, I know *a monster who can take a direct stab from a knife and only suffer a fraction of an inch cut*, he thought, envisioning a man in a bartender's outfit.

Izaya turned to the nurse and asked, "Do you suppose the newspapers and TV stations are talking about me getting attacked?"

"Hmm... Now that you mention it, I think TV King ran a segment on you in their *Scooped! Morning Star* program. They even mentioned your name. Why do you ask?"

"...Ah. I see. No, I just didn't want my friends to worry."

TV King, huh? That's a local affiliate of the Daioh TV network.

And the show she mentioned was a news program that Daioh TV ran nationally. Assuming that word of the attack had reached Tokyo by now, one concern occurred to Izaya:

If the incident was aired as part of this morning's news...

*   *   *

That's about enough time for the quick-acting types to start reaching this hospital here.

♂♀

May 6, 2:00 AM

The hospital was surprisingly quiet after dark.

Izaya silently waited in his bed.

Here we go. Will someone show up? Or will my guess be wrong?

He recalled all the bad karma he'd left behind up until the moment he was stabbed.

He'd fed the pair of Russians info and attempted to use them to eliminate two monsters who represented obstacles to him. He'd set up that animal in the bartender's suit to run up against the Awakusu-kai and forced the girl who had fused with the cursed blade to exit the stage.

While these spontaneous plots moved along, he flapped his wings like a bat, hovering between yakuza groups like the Awakusu-kai and the Asuki-gumi. It was possible that his manipulation of the Awakusu head's granddaughter had been exposed, too.

In addition to these things, an info broker tended to earn malice through his job. He had dirt on so many people that he couldn't begin to guess their number.

In essence, Izaya created nothing.

The information agents that made their business by dealing with the police or criminal groups were typically barkers for cabaret clubs or bar bouncers. The line of work was a suitable side gig for those who had an ear close to stories on the street—managers who swept up runaway girls, hostesses at nightclubs, and so on.

But Izaya was different. He made connections with those "part-time brokers" and occasionally made use of their services so that he possessed an information network that spread throughout the city like a spiderweb.

When useful information washed into his web, he found a way to profit from it. He could manipulate the mood of the city itself.

He didn't create anything.

He just found a way to make money.

Izaya understood what he was doing was deplorable, that he traded in rumors and stories and begged for cash in response.

But more importantly, he knew that even more deplorable types— who would happily fork over the money for that information for a chance to screw others over—were as numerous in society as grains of sand on a beach.

It was his personal business, but it was not the point of his life.

The point of Izaya Orihara's life was to love humanity—in a way that only he could manage or understand.

So, who's going to show up?

He couldn't help but grin, sitting in absolute silence, the hospital room lit only by the faint glow of the dimmed hallway lights and the stars through the window.

If it's him, he might have seen me on the news and run here on his own two feet, Izaya thought, his smile curling into a snarl at the thought of the bartender-vested monster. *Maybe this time he'll finally get the long prison sentence he deserves for rioting in a hospital... As long as I survive the incident, that is.*

If not him, maybe Anri Sonohara. At this point, she might actually be able to carve me up into pieces.

What if it's someone less expected, like Masaomi Kida or Namie Yagiri? Or perhaps those Russians.

And I can't count out the possibility of an Awakusu hitman...

Maybe no one shows up at all. I wouldn't mind. I could celebrate my own good fortune.

Sitting in his hospital bed, Izaya was full to the brim with excited expectation, like a child thinking about tomorrow's school field trip.

The wound on his midriff throbbed with each anticipatory pulse, but by this point, even the pain was just a bit of spice to heighten the sensations of the moment.

An hour later, when the first inklings of sleep finally began to creep into Izaya's brain, a fresh sound vibrated his eardrums.

Here we go.

This was not the pacing of the nurse on the night shift, but the careful, quiet steps of someone trying to hide their presence.

Not quiet enough, though. The sound echoed with a rhythm that Izaya's ears found pleasing.

I wonder who it is. I doubt it's him—*he wouldn't bother trying to sneak. And the Russians wouldn't be sloppy enough to make any sound at all.*

It was probably either an Awakusu-kai member or Masaomi, Izaya thought, right as the door to his room opened.

A shadow slid into the room.

"...?"

A young woman, her expression dark and foreboding.

But in contrast to her gloomy features, she glared at Izaya's starlit face with searing intent.

"I finally...found you..."

The note in her voice was complex: possibly hatred, possibly fierce joy at finding a fated rival.

"Uhhhh," Izaya replied, totally baffled.

"...Who are you?"

Ordi **nary A**

Rendezvous
Bolero

May 5, morning, Shinjuku

"...So, he never came back," the woman muttered as she watched the pot bubble away.

Through the rippling air above the pot, her hair shone, long and black.

Namie Yagiri stood in an apartment bordering Shinjuku's central park, thinking about the absent owner of the residence...

But the moment only lasted a few seconds.

"This stew turned out better than I expected. If he's not going to come back, I should take it to Seiji instead."

She tasted the broth of the dish. Namie's harsh expression softened and reddened a bit as she thought of herself and her lover Seiji hunched over the hot pot.

If judged solely on appearances, she would seem to be a woman with a childish side for her age.

But that was only if you didn't know the truth: that she was thinking about her brother.

—And that she wasn't thinking of familial love, but the carnal, lusty type instead.

Namie turned off the stove and reached for the TV remote.

She sat down on the sofa with graceful ease, stretching her legs and inadvertently exuding feminine beauty into the otherwise empty room.

On the TV, the morning news programs were just starting up.

What's with this? The TV in here is way nicer than the one in his other apartment.

She proceeded to glare lazily around the interior of the room. While she might have been acting like she owned the place, as a matter of fact, she'd only been there for fifty hours.

Ordinarily, she worked as an assistant to an info broker, out of an apartment located in a different building in Shinjuku. Now that office was empty, though, due to present circumstances.

The info broker took out this apartment as a refuge in case a certain man who wore a bartending outfit came after him—and now he was even hiding from Namie, apparently.

He was supposed to contact her at night, and even that hadn't happened.

"He can be surprisingly sloppy about certain things. Perhaps that bartender boy caught him and beat him to death," she muttered as she flipped through the channels. She stopped when it landed on a horoscope segment that she usually watched. Her expression went lustful as she imagined her brother's face.

The next instant, a familiar name came over the TV speakers.

"A citizen from Tokyo named Izaya Orihara was traveling alone when he suddenly collapsed, bleeding from his abdomen..."

—?!

An abrupt shock to her senses from an unexpected source.

Izaya...Orihara?!

Did she mishear, or was it a different person by the same name?

Her mind suddenly engaged and active, Namie listened closely to the newscaster.

"...the street of a shopping area near the train station. Witnesses claim they saw Mr. Orihara fall to the ground, bleeding. The victim is currently receiving treatment at a local hospital, where police say he had lacerations matching those of stab wounds. They believe it was a

random attack by a passerby. As Mr. Orihara recovers, we will wait for more detailed information..."

"Whoaaa..."

The chyron on the screen said, "Injured: Izaya Orihara." There was no photo to identify him, but it seemed pretty certain that the news report was about the very man whom she worked for. Even the kanji for his name were the same, and it was a strange enough name that all doubt was removed.

Still, the knowledge that her boss's name was all over the news didn't provoke any reaction other than pale cheeks.

He got stabbed.

She changed the channel. The other networks were all discussing some celebrity's love life or airing morning anime, so it didn't seem like a major national story.

Well, if they take it as just some squabble between thugs, it wouldn't be treated like a huge deal... And I guess that's not far off the truth.

Izaya had plenty of personal baggage. Namie was well aware of that after working for him all this time.

She wasn't particularly inclined to get involved in his personal business, but her employer getting into trouble wasn't a desirable outcome, either, so she tried to keep herself aware of information that might end up affecting her.

Still, there were so many possible attackers she could think of, the fact that he was stabbed didn't seem all that notable.

"..."

Namie's number was placed in his cell phone as a "pizza place," so she wasn't worried about the police calling her out of the blue based on that. Would they even bother to track down the individual numbers unless it turned into a murder case? Or did the police regularly go to those lengths for aggravated assault?

Oh... Does this mean really bad news for him?

Namie spontaneously wondered if what was a simple assault today might escalate into a murder attempt within the next few days. Now that the incident was news, and he was reported as being taken to a nearby hospital—what if that boy dressed as a bartender saw the report? What if some other person in an antagonistic position saw it?

Realizing that her employer's life might be in grave danger, Namie murmured...

"Well, in any case...I suppose I'm off work for the next few days."

She stood up, apparently satisfied with just that knowledge and nothing else.

Namie shut off the gas and put a lid on the pot that was still more than half full, her boss's face already banished to the realm of the subconscious.

In fact, it might not even have been in the subconscious—everything, including any concern for his life or death, might as well have vanished from her brain entirely.

"Seiji..."

She looked out the window blissfully.

...As if she saw her beloved little brother somewhere in the night skyline.

♂♀

May 6, midday, Ikebukuro, in front of an apartment building

There was a kind of shadowed, downcast beauty to the girl's face.

Her black hair shone in the sun, and her features had a whiff of foreignness to them. Not in the sense of being from a country overseas, but of something inhuman, like a painting.

Strangest of all was a large scar that ran around her neck. It looked like a surgical scar, as if to suggest that her head had once been severed and reattached.

When one stood next to her, the sight was jarring enough to make one wonder if this was some fantasy realm, rather than the real world. No doubt there were some people who had been enraptured by her upon their first viewing. However...

"Morning, Seiji!"

The bubbly, excited voice that escaped from her lips totally undid any effect her appearance created. It was the voice of someone without any troubles whatsoever, someone who believed that the entire world was in her corner.

Answering her call from the entrance of the apartment building, smiling briefly, was a young man. "Morning, Mika."

Seiji was dressed in his own clothes, not a school uniform, but one look at his face was enough to identify him as a high school student.

As for Mika, she looked young but often gave off an older appearance due to her otherworldly features. As long as she avoided speaking, that is.

"Where are we off to today? I'll go anywhere if it's with you!"

Innocent words. Childish voice.

It was the kind of silly, bubbly thing that people said when they just started going out, but as a matter of fact, Mika and Seiji had been a couple for over a year at this point. When they first met, she would speak to him in polite forms of speech, but at Seiji's request, she now took a closer, more natural tone of voice that was appropriate for their intimacy.

There was love, hope, and the rock-solid conviction of their relationship in her eyes. She looked as though she had just met the man of her dreams minutes ago.

By contrast, he was totally calm and collected and easily shrugged off her passionate gaze.

"Let's see… Wanna go catch a movie or something?"

Seiji gave her a weak grin and placed his hand on her shoulder.

♂♀

May 5, midday, café

The café located in the basement of the major electronics wholesale store exuded elegance. It often found itself host to meetings after work or lengthy, relaxed visits from friends and lovers.

A corner of the stately café buzzed with the excited voices of teenage girls.

"And as soon as he put his hand on her shoulder, Miss Harima just grabbed onto his and squeezed! And he said, 'Hey, it's hard to walk like this,' but his face sure wasn't complaining! It's incredible how they never get tired of each other."

"...Heat..." [They're so in love.] The gloomy-looking girl spoke to her glasses-wearing partner, who was all amped up. Aside from the difference in attitude, hairstyle, and the glasses, they looked completely identical.

Sitting across from the twins and listening intently was Namie, dressed in a business skirt suit.

"..."

She was silent as the twins described the events as excitedly as if they were their own personal experiences. Overwhelmingly silent.

"...Miss Namie?" asked the girl with the glasses, noticing something strange in her attitude.

There was nothing adding up to an expression on Namie's face. But her eyes were full of enough freezing force to stop anyone else in their tracks—enough to cause a trickle of sweat down the bubbly girl's back at least.

"What's the matter, Miss Namie?"

"Nothing. Please continue, Kururi Orihara and Mairu Orihara."

"Um...when you use our full names like that, it sounds a bit... intimidating."

"...Danger..." [I'm scared.]

The girls tensed and crept toward each other, sensing *something* swirling within the woman sitting across from them. The twin with the glasses—Mairu—decided to dispel the cold touch of fear by putting on a formal smile and continuing her report.

"After that, they went to the Metropolitan movie theater, where they're watching *Vampire Ninja Carmilla Saizou's Beginning* now! Or perhaps it's over already?"

"...A bit..." [Ten minutes left.]

"Ah," Namie murmured, lifting her coffee to her lips. "Thank you for all your observations and reports. Here is a token of my appreciation."

She slid a card over the table without emotion. It was a bank cash card.

"That shouldn't leave any traces behind, but I can't guarantee it's one hundred percent safe, so I recommend that you withdraw the entire balance and destroy it. The pin number is zero one six four. You'll find three hundred thousand yen, as we agreed upon."

"I've meant to ask," Mairu piped up apologetically, "do you really mean to give us all that money?"

"Of course. Why? Do you have some suspicions?" Namie replied, baffled at the idea. Even the questioning tilt of her head was captivating—but the cold nature of her face froze the spines of anyone who saw it.

"It just seems like a lot of money for watching what your brother does and telling you…"

"That is silly. For one thing, understanding more about Seiji is so valuable that it cannot be measured in currency. I merely arrived at the sum by calculating the amount of time that you watched him and converting what Izaya Orihara paid me during that period. It is not worth your concern."

The sisters leaned in and whispered to one another.

"Sounds like Iza is paying Miss Namie a hefty hourly wage."

"…Test…struggles…" [Maybe since it's his first time hiring someone, he didn't know a reasonable rate.]

Namie was close enough to hear what they said, but she gave no reaction whatsoever. She merely said, "I happen to think that I offer value greater than what he pays me. Watching over your capricious family is far tougher work than I ever imagined."

They replied, "Oh, you mean that someone stabbed him?"

She paused and then, seeming to realize something, asked the twins, "Have you…heard about what happened to Izaya?"

"…Station…morning…heard…" [The police called this morning to tell us.]

"Mom and Dad are both overseas for work, so the fuzz came to us first. I told them, 'He can rub some spit in the wound and be back on his feet in no time!' Then the lady on the phone yelled at me for talking about my own family like that."

Kururi admonished, "…Annoyance…" [Of course she did.]

But there was no pain or worry in her face about the fact that their brother was stabbed. Perhaps he really didn't mean that much to them.

For her part, Namie wasn't interested in her employer's family bonds, so she immediately switched topics. "Well, there's one thing I'd like to confirm about what you just reported."

"What's that? Just to clarify, my report contains subjective opinions, but no embellishment!" Mairu stated.

"What does Seiji…normally call her?"

"Huh?"

The twins looked at each other, not understanding the question. So Mairu gave her an off-the-cuff answer.

Without thinking, unfortunately.

"Umm, normally, he just refers to her as Mika. Usually, Miss Harima talks all polite with other people, in a way that gets kind of weird, but lately, she's been way more frank and blunt when she talks to him. According to another upperclassman we asked, they just started doing that as a mark of celebration for reaching a year together, so—" Mairu blabbed, until she was cut off by a strange sound.

Krakl.

With a dry crunch, the coffee cup fell from Namie's hand. It bounced off her knees and fell to the ground. Fortunately, she had finished the liquid, so nothing splashed out onto her clothes or the floor. But Kururi and Mairu were more focused on her hand.

Within her fingers was the snapped-off handle of the cup.

"I'm so sorry, ma'am! Are you all right?" stammered an employee, who rushed over at once. He assumed that something was faulty with the cup and that it had shattered on its own.

"…I'm fine. Nothing to worry about," Namie said, still cold. She gave the apologizing man the broken piece and sent him away, then lifted her cup of water.

Again, it was an elegant action, but Kururi and Mairu didn't fail to notice one crucial detail.

There were no cracks in the cup. She had broken off the ceramic handle with nothing but the strength of her fingers.

"Um, Miss Namie?"

"…Mystery…?" [What is it?]

The girls thought they sensed the cloudy presence of hatred in the air before them, and they pulled away slightly.

But Namie just looked past them, off into the distance at *something*, seemingly oblivious to them, and mumbled to herself.

"...by my name..."

"Huh?"

"..."

The words she then repeated were so obvious and self-apparent to the twins that they would have been funny if not for the powerful essence of madness behind them.

"Seiji's never even...called me...by my name..."

It was at that point that the twins noticed that her voice was full of both sheer murder and bottomless jealousy.

Both in levels that were far beyond the ability of the ordinary mind to comprehend.

♂♀

Thirty minutes later, theater lobby

Allow me to explain!

Carmilla Saizou is a vampire ninja!

He is the son of a vampire father and human mother, an agent of darkness with mastery over the ancient skills of the shinobi!

Despite his hatred for the vampire blood that runs in his veins, he prowls the shadows and fights the dark side of New Tokyo to preserve its peace!

In the first two movies, Saizou saved first New Tokyo, then Edo, and in this third movie, he's making his second trip through time—to medieval Romania!

There, he'll meet his father in his old human-hating days...as well as a brand-new enemy.

After a deadly battle that spans space and time, Saizou will find his own truth...

*   *   *

Seiji Yagiri looked up from the movie pamphlet often handed out with tickets in Japan and asked the girl next to him, "How was it?"

"It was sooo exciting! I got to sit next to you the whole time!" Mika Harima bubbled, winding her wrist around Seiji's arm.

"That wasn't what I meant." Exasperated, he turned to Mika and gave her a thin smile.

But his smile wasn't a reaction to the words she'd just said.

He was smiling *in response to the smile that her sculpted face reminded him of.*

♂♀

Seiji Yagiri was a man who lived in love.

He would take on a tank with his bare hands for the woman he loved. If he needed to tear out his own heart to keep her alive, he would do it without questioning (but only if he truly needed to).

Yet the target of this love was *not* the innocent but ominous girl clinging to his arm.

Technically, it was just her face.

What Seiji loved was the model face, the head that rested atop the body of Mika Harima. If, say, the woman at the ticket counter of the theater happened to have that same identical face, Seiji would just as quickly move on to adore her instead.

Was that really love?

Some might agree, if you claimed that you only loved sculpted heads.

But setting aside any deeper definitions of what love was, Seiji's individual case was a little bit more complex than just being infatuated with a woman's physical appearance.

He did not judge people entirely by outward looks. If a woman came along who was even more beautiful than Mika, it would not change his mind in any way.

It was through a great number of twists and turns, following a life driven mad by a particular woman's head, that Seiji was in his current relationship with Mika Harima.

And until the moment that he found the woman's real head, Seiji Yagiri would continue his pretend love.

He did it because looking at Mika Harima's face kept him from forgetting the *real* woman.

He believed that was love.

Mika Harima was a woman who lived in love.

And what she loved most of all about it was the concept of herself being in love.

So her partner's concerns were none of her own. She wouldn't think twice about breaking into her partner's house for the sake of living out her love. She wouldn't think twice about planting a hidden bug in her beloved boyfriend's apartment.

Even if Seiji fell in love with another woman, she wouldn't hate him for it.

Even if Seiji hurled hurtful names at her, she wouldn't despise him for it.

She would still love him, because her love was the most important thing in the world to her.

Her love was far, far, far more important than even the feelings of Seiji, the subject of that love.

So she would continue to love Seiji Yagiri—from the bottom of her pure-black heart.

Once, he had confessed his feelings to her: "I do not love you."

She could still hear the words in her mind, clear as day.

"But as long as you're around, I won't forget my love and dedication for her. Therefore, I accept your love. At least, until the day I get her back…"

And then he had embraced her.

Had done it willingly.

That was enough.

That was all the reason she needed to cherish Seiji Yagiri.

He accepts me. He accepts my love.

And so, she thought of the one that he truly loved through her.

The true owner of her face.

When she and Seiji found her, she would break that face into pieces right before his eyes and devour its every drop of blood, its every strand of hair. Then Seiji's love would truly be hers.

He might be furious. He might kill her.

She understood that. But it was an entirely trivial detail.

Mika Harima's thoughts on the matter were thorough and unblemished.

She had faith.

She believed that this feeling, which an ordinary person might consider insane, was actually the thing called "love."

As for the "real owner" of the face that featured so heavily in this boy and girl's love—well, it was not quite as mundane as one might think.

For the owner of the face was just the face itself.

It was a woman's severed head that still lived on today, even after being separated from its body.

♂♀

She was not human.

She was a type of fairy commonly known as a dullahan, found in Scotland and Ireland—a being that visits the homes of those close to death to inform them of their impending mortality.

The dullahan carried its own severed head under its arm, rode on a two-wheeled carriage called a Coiste Bodhar pulled by a headless horse, and approached the homes of the soon to die. Anyone foolish enough to open the door was drenched with a basin full of blood. Thus the dullahan, like the banshee, made its name as a herald of ill fortune throughout European folklore.

And the head that this knight carried was none other than the target of Seiji Yagiri's undying love.

A year ago, Seiji stole a test subject from the pharmaceutical company that his family ran. That subject was the very symbol of beauty that had been his object of worship from a young age—the dullahan's head.

After a series of events, he had to eventually give up the head. Instead, he received the presence of a girl whose face was reconstructed to look just like the dullahan's: Mika Harima.

Seiji ended up unable to tell the difference between the two faces—the head he loved and Mika's after plastic surgery.

The final blow was a mocking insult that arrived at the moment he realized his own inability to do so.

"Well, well. Looks like you couldn't even tell the difference between the real thing and a counterfeit."

He couldn't remember who had said it. Probably someone whom he didn't know very well. But those words became shackles that ensnared his love and tore it to bits.

"I mean, if we're being honest, that just shows you how real your love for that head is. Nice work, pal."

Seiji's love shattered in that moment.

But he didn't give up.

What was broken could be rebuilt.

So he let Mika stick around, to ensure that he didn't forget his love for the head—to serve as an admonishment toward himself.

Mika Harima was nothing but a conduit for Seiji's love for the head; she was but a terminal.

So for the sole purpose of confirming that his love was real, Seiji continued to play out a pretend relationship with a woman he did not love.

♂♀

Several minutes later, Ikebukuro

After leaving the theater, the couple decided to wander around the area. They started walking down Sunshine 60 Street toward Tokyu Hands, apparently without a specific destination.

Thanks to the extended holiday, the neighborhood was even busier than usual.

The crowds of a Tokyo metropolitan area took on different hues depending on the place. It was rare that they could be summed up and described with a single term, the way people talked about the fashion of Shibuya or the nerds of Akihabara, but even in Shinjuku and Ikebukuro there were distinct flavors to the crowds.

Seiji and Mika stood out somewhat from the general crowds here, but the excitement of the holiday easily hid what distinguished them.

"What did you think of the time paradox in *Saizou*?"

"Good question. It's the same thing I thought about the second movie; it didn't look like the future was changed that much, so what if it wasn't really the past he went into, but a parallel timeline? One that was close enough for Saizou to learn about his father's past... That was my takeaway. What did you think, Seiji?"

"Pretty much what you just said."

"Really?! Yay!" Mika giggled.

Without fanfare, he noted, "When I see stuff with monsters or vampires, I can't help but think of it," referring to something highly relevant to the two of them.

"...You mean the head?"

"Yeah."

Seiji didn't hesitate to bring up the topic, even out in public like this. He turned to face the girl walking next to him.

Mika Harima was no simpleminded fool. Seiji understood that.

His first impression of her personality was that of a stupid stalker who overrode people and never listened to them. But once they started going out, he realized that this was merely one crazy side of her and that she was also very cunning and intelligent.

Still, there were many mysteries about her.

Why me?

He had to wonder.

Yes, he had saved her and her friend from some thugs about a year ago. But he'd heard that even before that, she'd fallen in love with him at first sight during tests.

However. *However.*

This love at first sight, the gratitude of his help—whatever "fate" she might feel about their connection—were they all really worth risking anything and everything to make good on?

He had once split Mika's head open. He had tried to kill her.

And yet Mika Harima was still madly in love with Seiji Yagiri. She had put irreversible fake scars around her neck (albeit largely through coercion) and went under the knife to replace the face that she'd been given by her parents. She didn't regret any of this.

That was why it was so hard for Seiji to understand. If asked whether he could risk his life for love, he would answer yes. But he'd never had a broken arm or been in a situation with fatal consequences. Looking back, he thought the closest he'd ever been might be that moment when he picked a fight with the man in the bartender's outfit, but he'd been so worked up that he didn't have time to worry about his safety.

Could he, for example, continue to uphold his love through terrible torture? He believed he could, but there was no way to know the truth without actually experiencing it.

But he bet that Mika could probably keep loving him, even through torture. He just had a feeling.

Why?

If Seiji was a total narcissist, he might reach the conclusion that he was just *that* irresistible. Or if he fell in love with her, too, that doubt might never arise. If their relationship was half-hearted, he would grow afraid of her love.

Yet, to him, she was nothing but a conduit. So when viewed objectively, he was left with nothing but questions.

What does she see in me?

Seiji had pondered this question many times.

But every time his mind wandered down that path, he eventually remembered the *real* head and told himself that this question wasn't worth worrying about. Over and over again.

He got so tired of wondering that he just asked Mika outright. Predictably, she just answered, "Why, because it's you, of course!"

Now that they were on closer speaking terms, she would just say, "Because it's you!" but that didn't make it any better of an answer.

And today, after more than a year of the same thing, Seiji once again said, "I know I keep telling you this, but it's not you who I love."

"…I know."

"So why do you love me?"

"Because it's you, Seiji. I have no other reason."

Her answer was the same as always. Seiji sighed and decided to move on to a different subject.

"Sis has been missing for over a year, too… I'm guessing that she knows where the head is."

"…Are you worried about her?"

"Huh? Why would I be?"

"I mean, she's probably on the run from all kinds of people… Maybe she's in danger," Mika suggested, surprisingly thoughtful for once.

Seiji just grimaced and said, "She's not that helpless. She's tough—and evil." He didn't seem to want to get any further into the topic, as he cracked his neck and looked around them. "Let's get some lunch."

The street was packed with a variety of fast-food options, cafés, and coffee shops, as well as Taiwanese food and ramen down cramped side streets. Seiji patted Mika on top of the head and asked, "You in the mood for anything?"

"I'll eat anything you like, Seiji!"

This, too, was an utterly typical exchange.

I feel I read a passage in a book once that said men didn't like women who were too passive. Not that I really care. I'll accept the head for whatever personality it has, assuming it can actually talk.

Anyone else would have found that statement creepy, but Seiji merely followed his gut like always and picked out a direction for the meal.

"Maybe we should get some sushi for once."

They headed for Russia Sushi, right next to the bowling alley.

♂♀

Along the way, Seiji's eyes were drawn to a particular spot.

"…Hmm?"

He realized that a familiar face had just passed before his eyes.

"Ryuugamine. Is that you, Ryuugamine?"

"Huh?" replied a surprised boy with a youthful face. He glanced at Seiji and Mika and then smiled. "Ohh, Yagiri and Harima. Out on a date?"

"Yeah… Hey, what happened to your face?"

Their schoolmate at Raira Academy, Mikado Ryuugamine, was walking through the crowd with bandages and bruises all over his face.

"Oh, this? Nothing much… Just fell down the stairs at my apartment." Mikado laughed. Seiji sensed something amiss but judged

from the smile on the other boy's face that he wasn't going to get a straight answer anyway, so he decided to play along.

"Yikes. Well...be careful."

"Thanks," Mikado replied, still smiling benignly. "It's hard to believe that it's been over a year already, huh?"

"Hmm? Oh...yeah."

Seiji understood what he was referring to. A year ago, an incident had arisen having to do with the head, and Seiji had caused a great deal of trouble for Mikado. Technically, it was his sister who had put Mikado in danger—but Seiji decided to apologize for his part in whatever his past actions had brought about.

"Listen...I'm sorry about what happened."

"Hey, I didn't do anything. That was the Dollars as a whole."

"I see."

"And you and Mika are part of the Dollars now, so there's nothing to feel guilty about."

...?

That was when Seiji recognized what felt off.

Mikado almost never brings up the topic of the Dollars on his own.

The Dollars were a street gang that existed in Ikebukuro, repping the mysterious color of "nothing at all." Seiji knew that the other boy was a member of the gang. And based on the way Mikado acted and the places he found himself after the incident, Seiji knew that he was more than just a rank-and-file member.

But Seiji had no interest in questioning him and finding out those details. He wanted only to pursue his love. And while he still felt guilty toward the Dollars and Mikado, it didn't seem like learning those details was going to get him any closer to his desire.

Since then, they'd simply treated each other like classmates. Yes, there had been that strange hot-pot party at the Headless Rider's apartment they had both been invited to for some reason, but other than that, they weren't really friends. Just plain old classmates.

But even then, or perhaps because of it, Seiji had his misgivings. It was strange that Mikado had suddenly brought up the topic of the Dollars without being asked.

"Yeah...I can't forget what happened that night, either," Mikado said, unprompted. Who was he talking to? By the time Seiji decided that it was probably to Mikado himself, the other boy was already walking off and waving a hand.

"So long, you two. If you ever need anything, just let me know."

"Huh? Uh...yeah, sure," Seiji replied weakly, taken off guard.

"Mikado," Mika said, picking up Seiji's slack and removing her smile for once.

"Huh?"

"Don't ever make Anri cry, okay?"

"..."

"?"

Mikado fell silent, while Seiji was just confused. The stern look on Mika's face melted away, and she giggled and waved. "Well, see you at school, then."

"Er...right. Later."

Mikado smiled gently as he left, and then the couple resumed walking to Russia Sushi.

"...Did you think he was acting weird?" Seiji asked casually.

Mika nodded without batting an eye. "Yeah. He didn't seem like the usual Ryuugamine."

"And his face was all messed up. Wonder what happened," Seiji added, turning back to look in Mikado's direction.

Mika took him by the hand and started pulling him toward the sushi place. "Well, it's nothing we need to worry ourselves with! Shall we go?"

"Huh...? Oh, yeah, sure."

If anything weird happens, I guess I can ask him about it at school, Seiji decided and followed Mika away from Sunshine 60 Street.

But there was just a whiff of strangeness about the activeness with which Mika was leading the way, too.

♂♀

From the shadows, a lone woman watched the couple.

"...Seiji..."

Namie gazed at her little brother's back with an expression of ecstasy in her eyes. She was so relieved to see him looking hale and hearty that her body was undergoing a mild episode of intoxication.

Oh my God… How can he be so cute? And I'm only looking at his backside!

It wasn't an act; Namie really did feel dazzled by the sight of her brother's back. As a matter of fact, there were at least ten other young men of about the same age and with a similar hairstyle as Seiji in the vicinity—but within a single second of arriving, tipped off by the twins' report, Namie had correctly identified Seiji from the crowd.

Unfortunately, that also meant spotting the girl walking with him.

"…Mika…Harima…," she murmured, biting the inside of her cheeks. She used enough force to pierce the flesh just a bit, flooding her mouth with the tang of blood.

Namie narrowed her eyes, tasting the iron on her tongue.

This…is the taste of that little cat burglar's blood…

She was imagining the sensation of leaping out and biting Mika on the neck until her head ripped loose. Biting her own cheek was merely a way to make the illusion more real.

Namie trailed the couple, driven by an insane love for her brother and furious hatred at her romantic rival.

"Hey, pretty lady! You doin' anything right—?"

In the last several minutes, several men had tried to talk to her, either trying to pick her up or scout her for some modeling job or other.

"…Get lost."

In each case, Namie's expression froze, and she turned her lethal gaze on them with frosty precision. A man might react with hostility when treated with derision or annoyance, but Namie simply gave them a mechanical, truthful message of "You're not wanted here," without emotion.

In each case, the men instinctually understood. She was a woman who could kill out of habit, out of practicality, without even wanting to—and they were the only candidates in target range.

"…Whoops, coming through!"

Fortunately for these men, they were practiced enough to sense when a woman was trouble and could withdraw instantly to look for safer prey.

The process repeated several times as Namie tracked her brother and the girl, until she saw them go through the entrance of Russia Sushi—at which point she turned on her heel and strode back through the crowds down Sunshine 60 Street.

Meanwhile, her eyes burned with the flames of cold madness and lust as hot and sticky as magma.

$$♂♀$$

Russia Sushi

"Here, you get crab sushi. Eat raw, eat boiled, eat cooked. People good, town good, flavor good. Crab makes world go round."

"I think you mean 'cash.'"

"Not good for young person to talk about cash, cash, cash. You get cashed out. But if crab goes round, cash goes round. You trade my crab with your boss's cash. Round and round, merry-go-round. Russian crab and Japanese cash exchange. Revolving sushi. Good deal all around."

"..."

Seiji lifted the boiled crab nigiri to his mouth and shook his head.

Russia Sushi was famous for sticking out, even in Ikebukuro. It featured a traditional Japanese interior that clashed with Russian decor and was run by a white chef and a black waiter.

Seiji had been here with Mika several times now and was a loose acquaintance of the staff, but today was different.

"Who's that, Simon?"

There was an unfamiliar young white woman among them, dressed in a traditional Japanese uniform, like Simon. The combination was somehow mildly erotic, because even to Japanese sensibilities, her looks were undeniably attractive.

Yet there was an unpleasant pout on that pretty face, and she simply stood inactive in the corner of the restaurant. She stared into space with murder in her eyes, ensuring that no customer would have the courage to approach her.

"Oh, young master Yagiri, you like her? Her name Vorona. You take her to go, A-OK. Then you have girlfriend and mistress, one in each hand. Best to eat with those you love, makes everything taste good. Plus ten orders of sushi," Simon joked, but the woman was not amused.

"...Negative. I am under no obligation to sell my own flesh for the profit of the company. I request a boycott. But if your words are meant in the spirit of contract job, I confirm."

"Ohh, this is famous Japanese sexual harassment trial. Sexual harassment bad, no *sekuhara*. If you do *sekuhara*, then you do hara-kiri. And after cutting stomach, sushi all fall through hole. Our business go up in flames," Simon lamented as he returned to the kitchen.

Seiji continued to stare at the woman he called Vorona, until Mika tugged on his bicep, her cheeks puffed in comical anger.

"Stop that, Seiji. You're not supposed to look at other women!"

"Huh? Oh yeah," he said, but something weighed on his mind.

That's strange. Usually, she wouldn't care; she'd just say, "I'm not worried, because I'm hotter than her, anyway!"

I wonder if it's because she's foreign. The head has a foreign face, too... Maybe it's a sore spot for her. Probably not worth worrying about, though.

That was about the depth to which Seiji considered the strange, subtle change in his false girlfriend before he moved on to another thought.

After that, Mika continued the meal in her usual way, teasing and chatting with Seiji the whole while. She clung to him like a brand-new girlfriend, excited and naive, while he maintained an aloofness that was cool but never cold.

It was an odd, artificial mixture of personalities, but at a glance, they appeared to be a fairly close romantic couple.

Later, the woman named Vorona spoke to the chef about something and then slunk into the back with a nasty look on her face, but by that point, Seiji had stopped having any interest in her.

"...You know, I think it's incredible that Yuuhei Hanejima keeps doing these *Carmilla Saizou* movies. He's a big enough star that he doesn't have to stoop to doing that silly role, but they say he's already signed on for another sequel."

"What's the next one about? Is that where his rival Dracule Sasuke comes back to life?"

"That's the one. Y'know, for being such dumb movies, they get really great makeup effects from Tenjin Zakuroya. I really liked the way they did up Ruri Hijiribe in the first one."

"Aren't Ruri Hijiribe and Yuuhei Hanejima going out now?"

They continued their meal, engaging in simple watercooler talk.

"Even coming from a guy, I think Yuuhei Hanejima's a pretty cool, good-looking actor. I know not everyone loves the pair, but I think they suit each other."

"Well, I think *you're* way better than Yuuhei Hanejima," Mika interjected in typical fashion.

"Mika, your phone's ringing. Mika, your phone's ringing."

Suddenly, a ringtone recording of Seiji's voice went off somewhere in Mika's bag, and she rustled around and pulled her phone out of it.

"...You sure that ringtone isn't too creepy?"

"You think so? I don't mind it at all."

"When did you record me saying that, anyway?" Seiji grumbled. Mika looked down at the screen.

Unlisted number.

She narrowed her eyes, then pressed the call button anyway and held the speaker up to her ear.

"...Hello?"

And at the moment she answered the call, her holiday did an about-face.

"...Yeah. Yeah. Okay. Hang on."

Mika got up from her seat with a smile on her face. "Sorry, Seiji, it's a call from a friend. Mind if I go outside to take it?"

"Yeah, whatever," he said easily. She waved to him, exited the sushi restaurant, and stood to the side of the door to continue her call.

He watched her go, then glanced down at the sushi menu and thought to himself, *It's really rare for Mika to take a call from a friend. Is it Sonohara? You know, that reminds me—I seem to recall Sonohara and Ryuugamine talking about new cell phones recently.*

Speaking of which, I don't really get their relationship, either. I can tell that he likes her. I said something about that to him at the end of our first year, but I don't know what happened after that, if anything.

Mikado Ryuugamine was very close with a girl named Anri Sonohara, who was Mika's friend.

Their relationship was famously visible within the school, but it was hard to say if they were really lovers or not. They were close enough that a student who didn't know them that well might be surprised to hear that they weren't a couple.

But until recently, there had been another member of their group.

I suppose Ryuugamine would know the reason Kida left school.

Masaomi Kida was Seiji's schoolmate until he dropped out at the end of the last school year. They were in separate classes, so they'd hardly ever spoken, but Seiji knew that Kida hung around with Mikado Ryuugamine and Anri Sonohara all the time.

Some people said Kida had left due to the shock of the other two hooking up, but given how vague and uncertain their relationship continued to appear, there was a lack of evidence to support the rumor, and it soon died away.

But if Mika's got even a single friend, that would be Sonohara.

And even that girl had hardly ever called Mika on the phone. She recognized that his relationship with Mika had its own peculiar circumstances and was considerate enough not to bother Mika about the details—but that only made this call all the more suspicious.

After a while, the young woman came back into the restaurant. She wore an awkward smile, winked, and held up her hand sideways in apology.

"Sorry, Seiji… I agreed to help a friend with a problem, and now I've got to go meet them," she explained, bowing her head.

He leaned toward her and asked, "Are you talking about Sonohara?"

Maybe it's like that other time when they asked her to teach them how to cook fish the way she does, he wondered.

Mika beamed and said, "Yeah, that's right. She's got some kind of family thing to talk about. Honestly, I'd prefer to just hang out with you, but…"

"Listen, it's fine with me. I was thinking that you ought to treasure your friends a little more, in fact."

"Aww, really? As long as I have you, Seiji, I don't need *any* of my friends."

"Stop being macabre and just get on with it," he muttered.

Mika bowed again, smiled wistfully, and then announced, "I'll see you tomorrow, then!"

"Yeah."

She set down three thousand-yen bills on the sushi counter as she headed for the door.

"Oh, hey, I'll pay for it. Hey! Wait!" Seiji said, grabbing the bills, but she either didn't hear or simply ignored him as she left the building.

He was about to chase after her when the waiter returned with his order. "Hi, here your food, miso soup with crab."

Seiji hesitated and then decided to stay and finish his meal alone.

I can give her the money back tomorrow.

♂♀

Fifteen minutes later, Tokyo, warehouse

"…Hello."

They were on a block near the national highway route, distant from the shopping district.

After separating from Seiji, Mika made her way here, to a building labeled Yagiri Pharmaceuticals, Storage Warehouse No. 3. For being a warehouse, the building was surprisingly clean and orderly. In fact, from the outside it looked like nothing else but a research facility. The exterior was a pure white, with large gateposts like the entrance of a hospital.

But that was only in terms of the exterior. On the inside, it was—sure enough—a warehouse, with a central storage room the size of a small gymnasium, surrounded by hallways, a few airtight little rooms, a bathroom, and a small break room with running water.

The warehouse itself was split into sections with screens, each area containing a stock of materials—tools or pharmaceutical products—effectively carving the large room into a bewildering maze.

The warehouse floor appeared little used; spiderwebs gathered in the corners of the space, and tufts of dust and debris littered the floor. Light from the outside entered the building through the glass doors at the entrance, but the interior illumination was not on. Even the location of the switches was a mystery, creating an eerie gloominess to the structure—a far cry from the clean, updated image of an advanced pharmaceuticals company.

Near the entrance, Mika leaned forward and called out loudly and sternly, "Hellooooo?"

Her voice echoed off the hospital-like entrance. Yet there was no reception area of any kind, just a door to the main storage area farther on and walls of stacked cardboard boxes and other supplies in between.

Mika took a step inside and glanced down the hallways branching off in either direction, but there was nothing down them until they ended. It was as though this building had been completely removed from the normal routine of the rest of the city.

She headed carefully down one hallway to the open door leading into the building's center. But no sooner had she taken a step into the storage area than a loud clicking sound came from the antechamber behind her.

Mika spun around to see a woman standing before the glass doors that led into the building, locking them shut.

An elegant woman with long hair hanging down her back. Mika recognized her at once.

"I've been waiting… Or should I say, I'm afraid I've been keeping you waiting…Mika Harima."

Something in the way she spoke put Mika into a poetic state of mind. If ice could burn, it would emit the kind of air this woman spoke—such was the freezing cold burn of Namie's voice.

"I'm so sorry, my dear. You've been enjoying a very, very long dream…of the kind that can never come true for you."

Raw, overwhelming emotion was apparent to any who might hear that voice.

But Mika Harima was not frightened. If anything, she glared back at the woman with a challenge in her eyes.

*   *   *

"It's been a while...*Sister-in-law*."

grikk

grikk

grrk   *grik*

A strange sound emerged from the front room.

Mika recognized it as the sound of Namie's teeth grinding.

Namie stood before the glass doors. The light from the outside silhouetted her, shrouding her expression in shadow. Mika couldn't make it out from where she stood, but the facial expression made no difference. The teeth grinding was all the information she needed to understand that the situation was dangerous.

She was probably smiling. On the surface for sure, but it was quite possible that she was smiling with all her heart, too.

At least, that was how it seemed to Mika.

"One year..."

As a matter of fact, there *was* indeed a note of bliss in the words that next came from Namie.

"It's been one year and one month since Seiji left me. In that time, we've both had dreams to tide us over. I've been having a nightmare, and you've had the briefest, most ephemeral dream of fleeting pleasures... Oh, I'm sorry. Ha-ha, would an ignorant little girl like you even know what the word *ephemeral* means?"

"...Don't assume I'm uneducated."

"Why, I have a hard time imagining any truly educated, cultured person forcing their own fantasies onto Seiji and shamelessly picking the lock to his house," Namie retorted, her words dripping with sarcasm.

Mika merely chuckled and shot back, "I'm amazed to hear a line like that from the woman who was going to dump my dead body and then decided to give me plastic surgery for her own devices the moment she realized I was still alive."

"..."

"As a matter of fact, I'm quite grateful to you, Sister. Thanks to you giving me this face, Seiji and I are finally able to be together."

*   *   *

gcrakk

A louder crunch echoed off the walls this time.

They stood feet apart, but Mika could very nearly feel the boiling loathing of the other woman on her skin.

Unperturbed, *she tilted her head back* to offer a condescending challenge: "After all, *as long as I can love Seiji the way I want, I don't need education or culture.*"

The grinding was no longer audible. Namie unwound her arm from around her waist and held it up. "Don't you dare...call me 'Sister-in-law' again..."

In her hand, she held a shining silver object—surgical scissors.

"Don't you dare...say Seiji's name...without the respect it deserves!" she screamed and hurled the scissors.

They flew right at Mika's face like a particularly large dart.

The scissors cut through the air between Mika and Namie with incredible speed...

And then an ugly sound filled the space.

♂♀

It was the cell phone call that had summoned Mika Harima to this location.

"Hello?"

As soon as she answered the call in the middle of her lunch at Russia Sushi, the female voice on the other end had said, *"I want to talk to you in private about Seiji. I'd prefer if he didn't hear about this. Is that all right?"*

The caller gave no name, and Mika did not ask for one. She played along and responded in a breezy tone so that Seiji could hear.

"…Yeah. Yeah. Okay. Hang on."

Once she was outside the restaurant, the woman on the other end continued, *"I'm guessing you managed to fool him. You really are despicable, the way you can just lie to Seiji like that."*

"Says the woman who messed with my face for the express purpose of deceiving her brother," Mika replied, fully aware that she was speaking to Namie.

The other woman didn't miss a beat or take the bait. *"I didn't lie to Seiji. I loved him,"* she said, a bizarre excuse. *"If you want that head the two of you are looking for…I could give it to you."*

"Huh?"

"However…I want to talk to you in person first."

A lie.

Anyone who knew Namie even the least bit could instantly understand that she was lying.

"…Do you really expect me to believe that?"

"Listen, I'm not sure what to do, either… If I hand over the head to a foreign company, I have a guarantee that the police and Yagiri Pharmaceuticals' muscle will protect me…but I want that to be my final resort."

"…"

"But if I give Seiji the head, it will steal Seiji from me. I want to avoid that. If there's anything where our interests are aligned, it's that, isn't it? So…I want to discuss what to do with the head—without Seiji knowing about it."

Nothing in what Namie said was trustworthy. Nothing.

But Mika took her up on the offer, anyway.

As suggested, she came alone, without informing Seiji.

*   *   *

And now there she was, staring down the oncoming point of a pair of scissors...

But Mika was neither stupid nor ignorant enough to come without caution nor preparation.

Still, even though she was neither stupid nor ignorant, her choice of preparation was a rather odd one for a teenage girl.

Metal twanged awkwardly.

The next moment, the scissors were stuck in the ceiling, and a silver object in Mika's right hand reflected what little light there was in the entrance.

"...What's that?" Namie asked, glancing at the object.

"Isn't it obvious? You *did* receive an education, didn't you?" Mika mocked.

Namie snapped, "Of course I know what it is. The implication of my question was *why* you are carrying such a thing."

Her eyes were narrowed, staring at the tool in Mika's hand.

It was a trowel—the kind used in gardening, with a pointed tip. At first she'd thought it was a kitchen knife, based on the size and shine; but no, it was just a compact hand shovel.

The item was totally out of place in Mika's outfit, in this location and situation. And yet she had swung it out of nowhere, deflecting Namie's scissors in midair.

Why is she carrying that thing around? the other woman wondered. The question was only natural.

There were two women in an unoccupied building. One threw a pair of scissors, and the other deflected them with a hand shovel. The sequence of events was patently bizarre.

But the girl at the center of this abnormality merely grinned and said, "A part of me believed."

"?"

"I knew this was a trap, but a part of me wondered if you might actually have a good reason to give me the head. I mean, you're still Seiji's sister." Mika chuckled. But her eyes were not laughing. "Just by being related to Seiji, you have the gift of my unconditional trust. Isn't that great? You're so lucky! You should be much, much, much more grateful to him! You should be grateful to God. You should be very, very, very, very grateful that you were fated to be born in Seiji's family!"

"Enough jokes. I want to know why you have that trowel," Namie demanded.

Mika looked up at her and smirked. "Well...if I actually get the head, I'll need a shovel, won't I?"

"...?"

"I've been doing lots of tests, assuming that it's about the size of a watermelon. I packed meats and bones of different sizes and toughness inside, did some tests..."

"What are...you talking about...?"

There was no abnormality in the girl's voice. That was what helped Namie realize that she wasn't bluffing or attempting to rattle her with nonsensical threats.

Mika was speaking the truth, nothing more.

"I figured that an edge this big...would be about the right size. But I can't imagine the taste. *I can't imagine how a dullahan's head will taste.*"

A nasty, cold shiver ran down Namie's back. An ordinary person would have trouble instantly processing what the girl was saying. But Namie, who had already ventured into the realm of the abnormal, understood what she meant within seconds.

Because she knew that if *she* were in that position, she would do the same.

So, she's— Yes, I understand now.

"Are you claiming you intend to be one with the head? That's totally illogical."

Mika beamed, satisfied that the other woman understood her plans, and admitted, "That's right. But so what? What's your point?"

"...I have no point."

Namie Yagiri's frown softened somewhat. She took a moment to consider things.

Yes, she would do the same thing if she were in Mika's position. If Seiji loved nothing but it, then just getting rid of that head wouldn't be good enough. It would only become eternal within his own mind that way.

She had to *be* the head.

She would attempt to be one with the head, no matter how preposterous and illogical that might be.

Well...I suppose the difference is that I'd shave the head's face off and place it over my face instead.

In fact, Namie was in a position to do exactly that. The reason she wouldn't and hadn't was because she still had pride in her position as his big sister. She couldn't abandon all the love she'd built up that way.

It was this understanding of her own nature that made the presence of Mika Harima unforgivable to Namie.

"I need...to reassess my opinion."

She reached down to her waist belt, running her fingers over an object attached to it. Then she pulled it loose from its case, revealing an eerie silhouette to Mika.

"Before, I just assumed you were a pesky nuisance...but from now on, I've upgraded you to the level of *rival*."

In Namie's hand was an aged medical saw, its blade rusted here and there.

She took a crisp step forward and, like flowing water, accelerated toward Mika.

With the tool in hand as her weapon and her twisted love for her brother her source of energy, Namie Yagiri turned into a hunter, closing in on her prey of Mika Harima.

"But in either case...what I do to you will be the same."

♂♀

A few dozen minutes earlier, on a cell phone call

"Hello?"

"Hello, is this Dr. Kishitani? It's been a while."

"*Oh? Ohh, ohh! It* has *been a while! You're still alive—should I be congratulating you on that?*"

"...We can skip the pleasantries. I'd like to schedule an emergency surgery—can you come to Yagiri Warehouse Three? It's easy to get in there still because Nebula hasn't started clearing it out yet."

"*Goodness me, has someone shot you? You certainly sound well enough over the phone.*"

"...Actually, I'd like to request the same operation as last year. I want you to re-create a woman's face. It's the same girl as the last time, so it should be familiar enough, I believe?"

"*Uhh...I'm not going to ask about the circumstances. Is tomorrow night all right?*"

"You can't do it now?"

"*I'm afraid I'm off duty today. I'm not in Tokyo at the moment.*"

"Ah...that's too bad. She was unlucky."

"*...She was?*"

"Yes."

"If you don't show up, I'll be forced to carve up her face myself... and I'm guessing it will be quite painful to her."

"*And I suppose the humane thing for me to do is stop you?*"

"It's too late for you to do anything now, Doctor. But you were never the type to be concerned with things like this, were you?"

"*Well, in this case, that girl happens to be Celty's cooking teacher.*"

"Oh, don't worry about that. If my intent was just *killing* her, I wouldn't bother to call you."

Namie ended the call there but continued speaking into the dead receiver.

"However, on your express request...I can make sure her tongue and right hand still work."

♂♀

Present moment, warehouse interior

"Knock it off and play nice... I was planning to leave your tongue and right hand functional...but if you keep darting and sneaking around, I can't even guarantee that."

The piles of wooden crates and cardboard created a simple maze in the warehouse, like miniature stacks of shipping containers on a dock. Namie prowled among them with her bone saw, taunting and threatening.

"I'm an amateur at plastic surgery, you know."

They'd been playing tag for nearly ten minutes already.

Namie was on the prowl, reveling in her hunt like a monster.

After Mika just barely managed to block the first attack with her trowel, she knocked Namie over and escaped into the warehouse. Amid the gloom of the mazelike interior, lit only by the outside light coming through the open hallway, Mika's voice echoed, "I'm surprised! I would have assumed you were just coming to kill me!"

"If that were the case, I would have just piped in poison gas the moment you entered the building."

The queen of envy strode boldly, steadily, like the guardian of the labyrinth. In addition to the case for the saw, she had a number of other waist pouches equipped on her belt.

"I don't want you to disappear; I want you to regret trying to steal Seiji from me. Plus, if you go missing…Seiji might take it upon himself to search for you, won't he? He's kindhearted enough to do that… I don't want him to waste his time like that, but I also don't want to show him your dead body, if I can avoid it," Namie said, trembling slightly as she envisioned her brother's face. "He's just such a good boy… You can easily imagine him racked with grief over your death, even if you were just a stopgap solution. And I wouldn't want you to confuse that emotion with love."

"Ah-ha-ha-ha! Well, at least we agree that Seiji's full of kindness!"

"Don't you dare…use his name so casually," Namie menaced, her voice's pitch suddenly lowering. *She twisted and swung into a reverse roundhouse kick, aimed at a cardboard box on a steel shelf. The movement was as precise and deadly as a metal-cutting machine.*

The box shot off the other side of the shelf.

There came a short, sharp gasp from close beyond.

Damn, I missed.

Namie wasn't a master of any particular martial arts, nor did she have the brute strength of a fellow like Shizuo Heiwajima. But she had been trained in self-defense methods since a young age—and when her emotions got the best of her, she could employ her body's full potential to deliver lethal blows like this one.

As a matter of fact, she could have easily broken her leg. She'd be feeling the damage in her muscles and joints tomorrow.

But all that aside, Namie was not the type of fool to let her momentary opportunity escape.

She instantly launched herself off the floor and through the box-sized hole she had just created. It was not the superhuman movement of a gymnast or of a daring thief limboing through laser security, nor was it the sort of thing that an ordinary human would ever do without some amount of hesitation or preparation.

Namie could easily have significantly hurt herself in the attempt, but she was fearless, sliding across the long shelf and popping up to peer around the spot where she'd knocked off the cardboard box.

She's not here?!

But she had heard the gasp come from right around this area. It was only seconds ago.

She glanced down both sides of the makeshift hallway bounded by standing shelves of materials but found nothing.

Where...?

Her ears, laser focused by the tension of the scene, picked up the sound of something shifting, scraping. Not from the left, right, front, or rear—but above.

"...!"

She looked up and tried to leap out of the way, but it was too late.

"Hi-*yah!*"

Mika, who had held her breath and climbed the shelving after that kick to the cardboard box, leaped onto Namie from above.

"Hi-yah"? Who are you acting cute for, you little bi—?

"Ah!" Namie gasped as she was slammed to the floor. Mika was sitting atop her chest, practically straddling her. The skin of her thighs beneath the skirt pressed against the swell of Namie's breasts, soft flesh against soft flesh.

It would make for an erotic pose—if it weren't for the hand shovel held menacingly against Namie's throat.

"Don't move now ☆," the girl said impishly, staring down at the demon woman. She prodded her throat with the tip of the trowel.

Namie's chest rose as she inhaled, rubbing against Mika's thighs through her shirt. The girl on top grimaced and noted, "You're hiding more under those clothes than I thought, Sister-in-law. Ha-ha!"

But her eyes were not laughing. Or rather, they *were*—but with a tinge of madness that was a far cry from ordinary good humor.

"So, how about it? Are you going…to tell me…where to find the head?"

Bit by bit, the end of the spade prodded harder into Namie's throat. Despite being in danger of losing her life, her first instinct was to offer praise: "I'm…impressed. I didn't think you were physically capable of this."

"Let's just say I've had experience climbing up apartment building walls and over fences."

"Now you're just bragging about your criminal record. Why don't you save your stories for a blog? Then you can get flamed, tell Seiji you're leaving him, and kill yourself," Namie spat mockingly.

Mika merely put more weight on the blade. Bit by bit, bit by bit. But suddenly, the pressure stopped, and the shovel fell out of her hands.

"Wha…? H-huh…?"

The tool rolled off Namie's throat to clatter against the floor of the warehouse.

"Why…can't I…squeeze…?"

"About time it started working," Namie grumbled. She held her left hand up so Mika could see. It was holding an object, likely taken from one of the pouches on her belt, just like the rusty saw.

"It's a painless injector I bought from Nebula a while ago. You didn't feel a needle, did you? Maybe more like…being grabbed by fingers trying to pry your leg away?" she taunted, tossing the injector onto the floor.

Powerless to stop itself, Mika's body toppled and rolled to the left, allowing the other woman to switch places with her.

"That's an old muscle relaxer I cooked up years ago. Don't worry—it won't kill you," Namie said, taking a seated position over Mika's waist so she could stare down at the girl. "What a horrid, hateful face you have. That doctor did good work," she murmured, stroking Mika's cheek.

"Ah..."

"Now, out of curiosity...how far have you and Seiji gotten?" Namie asked suddenly. It was the kind of question a close girlfriend would ask another teen. Only in this case, there was no curious, excited grin on her face—there was no smile at all.

"Please...don't make me say it out loud," Mika said in embarrassment.

"Have you...kissed yet?"

"..."

Mika merely looked back at Namie and then averted her eyes again.

"...So you have," the older woman said, taking the girl's response as confirmation.

"S-so...so what if I— *Mmph?*"

Namie leaned closer *and covered Mika's mouth with her own.*

"Mm! Mmm?!"

Mika tried to struggle, to flop her limbs around, but her body wouldn't take orders. After several seconds that felt like an eternity, Namie slowly pulled back. Her eyes were cold, full of hatred and disgust.

"I cannot stand the thought...that your face still bears the sensation of kissing Seiji. I feel sick doing this with another girl, but focusing on the fact that I'm indirectly kissing *him* almost puts me in a trance..."

Namie's mouth curled into a mocking smile, triumphant now that she had paralyzed her opponent. Then it took on a crueler note, and she pulled a bottle of medicine from another pouch.

"You know, I could have just carved it off with the bone saw," she said, holding up the unlabeled brown bottle, "but instead, *I think I'll use this fast-acting solution designed to melt human skin off without being fatal.* It's not my own formula, but it's just so hard to work with sulfuric acid without killing the patient, you know?"

"..."

"Whoever made this sure was a sicko...but it seems like the perfect medicine for *your* problem, no?"

There was no bluff, no threat in Namie's eyes—only truth.

Mika instinctually understood that the woman was about to

obliterate her face. But without being able to control her body, there was very little she could do to protect herself.

"Go on—cower in fear. I want to see that face of yours twist and contort with terror," Namie taunted, holding the bottle over the girl's head. But Mika did not scream or beg for mercy.

Namie sighed and went for the bottle's lid. "Do you have any last words while you've still got that face?"

Was that question meant to be an act of mercy or merely a demonstration of her superior position in the situation?

In either case, that question succeeded in drawing a *macabre* answer out of Mika Harima.

"*Ephemeral* and *fleeting* are words applied...to the vicissitudes of life. The rise and inevitable fall of all things."

"...Huh?" Namie squawked, pausing in surprise.

Mika smiled lazily up at her, so easygoing that it might have been the effect of the muscle relaxant, and it was in that tone of voice that she continued, "When we first...came into this building...you asked if I knew the meaning...of the word *ephemeral*. Well...I do know it. I know...a whole lot of things..."

"...And? Is that your final statement?"

It was just empty bravado. One last act of futile defiance.

Namie knew it was so. She wanted to believe it was.

She wanted to believe that the rising foreboding within her was nothing more than a figment of her imagination.

It took only seconds for Mika to shatter this futile hope.

"*Kanra...is Izaya Orihara.*"

Huh?

For a moment, Namie couldn't process what she'd just heard.

Kanra was the username that her employer Izaya used to interact with a specific chat room online.

Why would she mention...?

Then she paused.

Wait...how does this little bitch know Izaya's username in the first place? And has she ever...even met Izaya...?

"Tarou...is Ryuugamine."

"..."

"Setton...is Celty. Saika is Anri. Bacura is Kida. Mai and Kuru are Izaya Orihara's sisters, Mairu and Kururi."

This time, an undeniable chill ran through Namie's body.

Mika continued, her smile beatific, "And the username that both Izaya Orihara and you use when manipulating people...is Nakura."

"Wait..."

"Ryuugamine is the founder of the Dollars... Anri is possessed by a demon blade named Saika... Kida is the leader of the Yellow Scarves. But I suspect that none of the three is aware of the others' secrets."

Namie wanted to stop her, but now *her* body wasn't reacting. Was it instinct? Curiosity? Or just plain fear?

"The people who tried to hurt Anri yesterday and the day before... are a pair of Russians...Vorona and Slon...which mean 'crow' and 'elephant,' respectively. Izaya Orihara...hired them..."

How does she know this? Namie wondered. This creeping question eventually made every muscle of her body tense. *How much does she know?*

"Slon's connection to Izaya Orihara...is deeper than Vorona's. So Izaya heard about the Awakusu-kai's contract for Slon through him... and tried to entrap Shizuo Heiwajima. Someone stabbed him last night...and now he's in the hospital."

"...!"

Every single sentence was a definitive blow.

The last one was something Namie herself had only learned this morning—but *none* of it should have been in Mika's personal range of information.

"How...do you know these things?"

"Don't be silly... It's the same way...as always. Do you know...how cheap...and incredibly small bugs can get...nowadays? So I've...been placing them around...all the people who are likely...to get involved with Seiji. And I know a few things...about hacking..."

"...!"

"Izaya Orihara was the only one...who found the bug right away... but as long as whomever he talks to on the phone is bugged...I can still hear from him… Shall I reveal some things that don't involve you? Like last night, Mikado took a ballpoint pen, and…"

"Enough. Be quiet."

Planting bugs…? That can't be, Namie thought. She was frozen in place.

"What do you think…? I know lots of other things…such as the fact that you and Izaya…are also connected to the Asuki-gumi…"

"This…this can't be… You've never shown any sign of this before… In fact, if you always knew all the things you just said…you could have stopped them from happening!"

"Huh…?"

"The stuff with your friends! When that idiot Izaya led your friend on and screwed everything up…if you knew all about that—in fact, if you knew about Saika!—then you could have helped avert all that disaster! That ugly business! Before Masaomi Kida got hospitalized!"

"…"

Mika looked just a little bit sad. "Anri doesn't know…that I know," she said. "I don't think she's aware that I've been brushing up on her and Ryuugamine…the same way that I planted a bug in Seiji's room."

"But…that shouldn't matter…"

"If I told her that I knew everything…and helped her directly…that would mean getting personally involved in all that *mess*. It would be one thing if that was just me. I don't care about Anri and Ryuugamine being disgusted with me or getting arrested. But…"

She closed her eyes. That brief pause was all Namie needed to understand what she meant. Sure enough, the answer was as expected.

"If Seiji learned about Ryuugamine's secret circumstances, he might claim he owed that boy a favor and get involved with it… He mustn't know. Seiji might seem brusque and aloof at first…but at heart, he's extremely kind. Just like the time he saved me and Anri from those thugs…"

"…"

"So…I decided to learn and learn and learn and learn and learn and learn and learn about everything, even the people around him. So that I could make sure Seiji doesn't get involved in any of the danger they pose…"

Mika fell silent. Namie said nothing for a while, too. Silence fell upon the warehouse, as if time had frozen.

*　　*　　*

But…

"…I understand how you feel. And I understand now that you are far more capable than I ever gave you credit for…and far more abnormal," Namie murmured, unstopping the glass bottle.

Mika glanced at it, smiled, and then thought, *I wonder, if I blow really hard when she tips over the bottle, will some of the liquid splash back on her? That way I can take her down with me… Actually, never mind. Seiji would be sad if a family member was terribly hurt.*

Meanwhile, Namie slowly twisted the cap on the bottle. She had no idea what selfless thoughts were running through Mika's mind, but even if she did, it wouldn't have stopped her hand.

And yet, just at the moment that the glass bottle was about to open, Namie *did* stop. Not of her own will—but because a very familiar hand suddenly reached in to grab her by the wrist.

"…That's enough, Sister."

"S…"

The moment she heard the voice, Namie felt that her heart might stop as well.

Her shock might have been from haste, joy, or twisted love—or perhaps all three.

"Seiji!"

"Seiji?!"

Both women were stunned.

"Why…?"

Why is he here? Mika wondered—but Namie had no doubts whatsoever. She cast the bottle aside, stood up, and clenched Seiji's body tight.

"Seiji…oh, Seiji! I'm so glad…I'm so glad you'll still call me 'Sister'!"

"Ow, ow— Sis, you're hurting me," he said, prying his way loose of the affection. "Are you all right, Mika?"

"Y-yes…"

"I see. That's good," he said simply, then turned to Namie. "Sis…"

"S-Seiji…?"

Gone was the demonic possession from just moments ago. Now Namie gave him a look like a puppy caught in the rain.

He sighed and muttered, "I don't know what happened here…but I think you understand you crossed a line."

"Um…"

"If you had damaged Mika's face just now…I would have hated you for it."

"…!"

Namie knew that. She was prepared to undertake her plan and suffer that consequence. But as soon as she heard it from his own mouth, she realized how brittle her determination had been. Terror ran through her.

"H-how long have you been watching…?"

"…Since about the moment you kissed Mika."

"…!"

If anything, it was Mika who looked shocked at this. The fact that she had known all the secrets of Mikado and the others had *itself* been a secret—from Seiji. And now he had heard all about it. He knew that she had bugged not just him, but all his friends.

"Ah…aaaah…"

"I saw you two kissing, and I had no idea what was going on, so I kept watching…and then it seemed like things were getting dangerous, so I stepped in to put a stop to it," he said. His expression was dark, just like the warehouse itself, so he could have been exasperated, or he could have been mad.

Both Mika and Namie looked away uncomfortably. Eventually, Namie broke the silence to ask, "H-how did you know where we…?"

"I left the sushi place and went home…and I met Sonohara out in front of that old curio shop that went out of business."

"Huh…?"

"I asked her, and she said she hadn't called you. So then *I* called you and got your voice mail, and I started getting worried. I called everyone we knew, and that got me nowhere…so eventually I got desperate and tried the people we met at that hot-pot party…"

Seiji paused, scratched his cheek, then continued, *"Dr. Kishitani said you'd probably be here…"*

Namie suddenly pictured the face of the man she'd talked to no more than an hour ago.

That…that four-eyed freak! I swear…I'll get rid of him one day—along with that Black Rider!

She began to plot how she would get back at the black market doctor, magma bubbling in her heart—when something covered her raging, quivering lips.

—?!

Her sight went black. It felt like something was touching her cheeks and nose as well. She heard Mika gasp much louder than before.

…?

Suddenly, light came back—and she saw Seiji's face, pulling away from hers.

"See? It's really unpleasant to have something like this happen from a person who isn't your lover, right? So you ought to apologize to Mika————besides————since way back————that's—to female friends of mine————and you're always————"

Less than half the words that Seiji was saying were reaching Namie's brain.

…?!

Because she suddenly realized that the sensation she'd felt was a kiss from Seiji.

…!—?!—?—!—!—?!

The next thing she knew, Namie Yagiri was running from the spot.

"Huh?! Sister, wait! Where's the head—?!" Seiji called out after her, but she was already out of hearing range.

Impulses exploded within her, fiercely pumping from her heart and through all the muscles of her body.

Like a living engine, Namie Yagiri could not help but sprint at full speed for the next five minutes, before the muscles collapsed with fatigue at last.

♂♀

Five minutes later, Ikebukuro

"Why are you so angry?"

"I'm not angry."

"You are angry."

Seiji and Mika were arguing as they walked away from the Yagiri Pharmaceuticals warehouse. Technically, *he* was the one walking, carrying her on his back and hoping to hail a taxi while she recovered from the effects of the drug. But something was wrong with her attitude.

"Fine, fine, you aren't angry. At least tell me what I did."

"...You have no idea how a woman feels, Seiji," she said, turning her head so that her cheek rested against his shoulder. "I know that you really love my face, not me...that you love the real head...but that just makes it even more important if you're in love not to kiss your own sister..."

Mika never cared how much Seiji spoke to other women, but for some reason, her way of thinking was different at this moment. Was it because this was Namie Yagiri, the woman who declared herself an official rival for his love?

...I'm the worst. He learned my secrets; he should be far more angry with me *than the other way around...*

She felt disgusted at the way she was taking it all out on him. She buried her face into the middle of his back, ready to let the tears flow—

"I didn't."

"...?"

He openly admitted, "When I grabbed her face and pulled it closer, I put my fingers in between our mouths, just like this."

He held out two fingers and laid them sideways over his lips, then craned his neck and wondered, "For some reason, she assumed it was a real kiss... Based on the way she raced out of there, it must have really creeped her out. Funny, given how much she used to hug me..."

Mika's mouth was hanging open in shock. Eventually, she closed it and scolded, "Even still...that's terrible."

"Really? It is?"

"Yes. This sort of thing doesn't work on logic," she said, practically sulking.

"Ha-ha!" He couldn't help it.

"…What's so funny?"

"You finally did it."

"…Did what?" she asked, looking up.

He glanced over his shoulder at her and happily explained, "Normally, you just go 'Yeah, yeah!' and play along with whatever I say. So this is…kinda fresh."

"Seiji…"

"Plus, there have been lots of surprises today."

"…!"

Mika tensed. She'd been placing "spies," so to speak, on all the people Seiji knew as a tool to keep him out of danger. It was an action she didn't want him to know about, a side of her that even she knew was abnormal.

Mika Harima did *not* think that sneaking into the home of her beloved and placing bugs there was abnormal. It most certainly *was*, but not by her standards. However, she did understand that spying in this manner on people she did not love was abnormal by most people's standards.

Only she knew where her arbitrary, vague boundary between what was normal and abnormal lay—but what mattered now was that Seiji had learned about the thing she herself recognized as abnormal.

"Umm…"

She knew she had to say something, but no words came. Normally, she could talk about her love for him without ever running out of words, but now she found herself at a loss.

Thankfully, he spoke before she needed to.

"Sorry."

"Huh?"

"I don't try to pretend I'm a saint or anything. I'm just nosy. If I find out someone I know is in trouble, I suppose I might be inclined to stick my nose into it, too."

"Seiji…"

Why…? Why is Seiji the one apologizing?

She tried to say something, but once again, Seiji filled the gap.

"But…I'm not going to deny what you did for me, Mika."

"…"

"I'm starting to lose my grip on what exactly love is. All I know is that I love the head. I can't explain it. There's no logic to it. That's all I can say. I don't love you, and I only care about my sister as my sister—whatever she happens to feel."

"Yeah…I know."

She'd heard that speech many times before. His words were unbearably direct, but there was no lie in them.

After a while, he continued, "But the one thing I won't do is deny you. I might try to stop you, but I won't deny your thoughts. I respect your love. I just might not accept it."

"…!"

"If you caused trouble for someone else out of your love for me…I don't have the right to stop you from doing it. I heard you mentioning Ryuugamine's name and some weird words like *Kanra* and *Saika* or whatever—but I'm not going to worry about it."

He doesn't love me.

"You can tell me the details of that stuff later. Then we can discuss what we should do. After all, maybe something in all that trouble you don't want me to get involved in has a connection to the real head."

"…Right."

But he'll allow me to love him.

She nodded with a smile, and he sighed. "And despite all this selfish stuff I just said, somehow you still love me. What is it about me, anyway?"

The same question as always. But today, Mika had a different answer than usual.

"I'll tell you if you decide to love Mika Harima!"

"…Can I love you as a friend?"

"No, only as a lover."

"Then I guess I'll never know the answer."

Mika could pour all her love into him. That was enough for her.

What she truly cared about wasn't Seiji's heart. It was her own love for him.

It was an abnormal girl's eccentric love.

On the other hand, Seiji's lack of love for her and his acceptance of that abnormality *also* made him a resident of the abnormal
side.

For now, Mika felt that her love was blessed and celebrated.

For now.

Seiji shuffled through the town with Mika on his back, the sun making its slow descent toward the horizon. They continued their nonsensical discussion while ignoring the curious gazes of onlookers,
existing only in their own little bubble.

"Still can't move your limbs?"

"Nope."

"Liar."

"Yep."

"Whatever. Guess I missed the chance to ask her...where the
head is."

"I don't think she even knows anymore."

"...Maybe. Maybe that Izaya Orihara you mentioned has it. I've
heard that name in rumors before—maybe I've actually met him
somewhere. I could try finding out where he lives and sneaking
inside."

"There's no need to do that."

"Huh?"

"I've found three different apartments Izaya Orihara has and snuck
inside them multiple times...but I never saw any heads."

"...Oh. Well, there goes that option."

"Yep."

"Also, I don't think sneaking into people's homes is a good idea."

"Yep."

"...What would you have done if you found the head before me?"

"Eaten it."

"What?"

"If I become one with the head, then you'll love me, won't you?"

"Probably not. In fact, it's pretty much impossible in the first place."

"Why do you say that?"

"Because I'd stop you."

"By killing me?"

"Yeah."

"I knew it."

"...Do you hate me now?"

"Huh? Why would I?"

"Never mind."

"What about me? Not my face, but Mika Harima? You hate me now?"

"Not really..."

"Then...you love me?!"

"Not really..."

"Aww..."

"Don't 'aww' me."

"Okay, I was kidding. That was a fake 'aww.'"

"Wow, you gave up fast."

"..."

"..."

They vanished into the bustle of the city, continuing their endless conversation.

Her love was abnormal.

His sister's love was abnormal.

But in a way, the boy who bore their love and shrugged it off without batting an eye might have been the most abnormal of all.

The city of Ikebukuro accepted even this abnormal love triangle, playing the same tune it always did.

Swallowing them into its grand flow.

In ways slow, gentle, and majestic.

♂♀

Night, Shinjuku, apartment

In the usual apartment, its owner still absent, Namie took a shower.

"Seiji..."

How many times had she murmured that name today? It had been at least a hundred times during this shower alone. She pressed her lips and then clutched her body.

I suppose that counts as the first time I've ever kissed a man…

The qualifier *kissed a man* either meant she was disregarding her prior kiss with Mika or that she had experienced it with other women in the past—but in any case, there was nothing in her mind but the image of her beloved brother now.

She let the cold water wash over her, trying to chill the burning fervor of her flesh. If she didn't, her very sense of reason might crumble into ruin.

Seiji…

"Ha-ha."

Seiji!

"Ha—ha-ha, ah-ha… Ah-ha-ha-ha… Ah-ha-ha-ha-ha-ha-ha-ha-ha-ha…"

Maniacal laughter spilled out of her mouth as his name repeated and echoed in her mind.

There was a saying that love lasts three years while marriage gets stale in three days—but Namie's love for her brother would never get old.

There was a reason for that, of course; loving her brother was as natural as breathing for her. No human being grows "tired" of breathing.

And just like breathing, Namie could not survive without loving him.

She would continue living, subsisting on her love for her brother.

She would do so tomorrow and the day after that…until the day Seiji no longer existed. Perhaps even beyond that day…

"Seiji…"

She exhaled that breath of desire, the heat of it dissipating into the Ikebukuro night.

Ordinary B Outcast Concerto

Six years ago, Ikebukuro

What is this?
 What am I looking at?

He was a tremendous fighter.

Even among the mobsters that the government euphemistically termed "violence groups," he wielded a violence that was second to none.

The rest of society knew him as a strongman, and he believed in that strength.

He had thrived in the shadows of modern society on his might alone; he had made a living just by being good at fighting. He could be proud of that life.

New-school "intellectual" yakuza, the Anti-Organized Crime Law... These changes were the wind; they meant nothing to him.

It was important to adapt with the times, but the law of the street still reigned supreme: If you didn't command respect and fear, you were done.

All he could do was handle things the way he knew best.

A few years ago, some men who worked for a fellow in his line of work—a rival of his, some said—were beaten up by a kid in a bakery.

He felt pity, mirth, and anger all at once. It had to be a joke. He didn't believe the story.

Later, that very kid would don a bartender's uniform and become a kind of urban legend—but the man couldn't have known this at the time.

So he decided to keep fighting, to show his companions how a *real* man fought.

Fight, fight, fight.

He sought to gain everything he could see through sheer violence alone.

He knew it was impossible. But he didn't stop.

He couldn't stop.

No stopping the endless impulse from within.

The intoxication of violence.

There was no way not to test the technique honed by true experience, the muscle built and forged.

No way not to display it.

Even if nothing but ruin lay ahead, he was determined to use his strength exactly as he desired.

Then, one day…

He met a monster.

What the hell is this?

It was *not* the oft-rumored Headless Rider on a silent motorcycle—but the more recent phenomenon of a slasher with a katana.

What am I looking at?

No one knew about it at the time.

They couldn't have known.

Even now, only a scant few aside from him actually knew the truth.

Is this…real life?

This slasher was a shape-shifting monster in the truest sense of the word.

A red-eyed monster sprouting katana blades from all over its body, leaping and darting like no human being could.

He didn't know the monster's name.

"Damn you..."

He didn't know the name of Saika, the cursed blade that loved humanity.

"What the hell are you, dammit?!"

He received no answer.

The tip of the monster held in that red-eyed human's hands cut through a part of his body.

And then time passed...

♂♀

May 4, late night, Tokyo, club

A club pulsing with lascivious sound and light.

It was classified as a "café" for the purposes of the Adult Entertainment Business Act, but in reality, it was closer to a nightclub or a disco of the previous era. The proprietors rented out the space every night to a different production company, hosting events of all kinds.

Tonight, young men and women danced and writhed on the dark floor, indulging in a variety of pleasures, their bodies and minds stimulated by the insistent pounding of the bass subwoofer.

Some danced to the beat of the music, some watched the dancers, some savored their drinks and the tunes, and some let their excitement move them to call out to members of the opposite sex.

All these activities and more were captured in vivid detail by the pulsing, strobing light system. But in addition to all the above, there were some people in this particular club who carried out their own activities, unaffected by the overwhelming stimuli.

Inside the men's bathroom, the club's sound system was muffled.

"Hey…you're holding, right?"

"I brought the money for it. Okay? Okay?"

Young women in heavy makeup hissed impatiently. They felt no hesitation or anxiety about being in the men's room.

Facing them were three tough-looking men. Striking tattoos were visible around their collars, and while they weren't any older than their early twenties, they surrounded the younger girls with an eerie, menacing vibe.

The slimmest of the three men leaned in with a wide smile. "Yeah, yeah. Don't worry. We've got the stuff."

Relief flooded over the girls' faces. But there was little color in their skin, which was slick with a sheen of messy sweat.

"The problem is, you know how hot this stuff is right now. It's hard to come by on the street. You know how it goes, right? So I'm gonna keep the price the same, but this is all you get," he said, producing a ziplock plastic bag and dangling it in front of the girls. There were white pills inside.

One of the girls reacted with despair. "But…that's only half the usual amount…"

"Actually, to tell the truth, I was saving this for a VIP customer, but you girls look really desperate, right? And we hate to sit back and do nothing for cute girls who really need help."

"…Fine. Then…I'll pay double…just gimme the normal bag," she gasped, not even able to complete a full sentence in one breath. She was swallowing quite often, as if desperately thirsty.

One of the men rubbed each of the girls' cheeks in turn and laughed. "Don't worry—we'll help you find some work to pay it off. Don't look so gloomy, sweet cheeks."

The man with the bag waved it in front of their faces—like dangling a carrot in front of a horse.

But this carrot was snatched up by a sudden cross breeze.

The sound of flushing water came from one of the stalls.

"?"

The men glanced over at it, annoyed.

It was the stall closest to the door, but it had been empty when they first came into the bathroom—or so they thought. And unbeknownst to the girls, the men had two friends on guard outside the bathroom to tell anyone who wasn't a client or a friend that the janitor was working inside.

"…"

Perhaps it was one of those guards who used the stall, but they hadn't noticed anything before this point. Not even the sound of the door closing.

"C-come on, gimme…," said one of the girls.

"Shut up," one of the men commanded, watching the door cautiously.

The next few seconds felt many times longer. Whoever it was, he was probably police.

If it was just an ordinary visitor to the club who managed to wander in while the guards weren't paying attention, he would be easy to threaten or drive off. But they hadn't even heard any toilet sounds, nor the unrolling of paper. Whoever was in there simply flushed the toilet, nothing more.

When the door began to open, that confirmed that whoever was in there wasn't flushing to mask the sound of his business. In other words, he had gone into the stall, went completely silent, then flushed—but why?

They weren't inclined to think that he merely spat into the bowl. And the very presence of an unannounced visitor was quite far from the expected for them. This was their turf, the place they used to peddle an illegal drug—and their experiences had taught them to be wary of what just happened.

"Hey. Who's there, huh?" one of the thugs threatened, inching closer to the open stall door.

It opened silently, and a man emerged.

Contrary to what they had been afraid of, he was not an investigator. But neither was he just a normal person who had wandered into trouble.

"Hey."

He was rather odd.

"Look at you young fellas. All worked up, doing your thing."

A tall man dressed in a flashy suit. Somewhere in his thirties, they gauged. Not young, but not yet middle-aged, either. He was slender and wiry with a scar on his face—not a pushover by any means. There were expensive tinted glasses on his nose and an ornately designed walking stick in his hand; he was like a memorable character from an old movie, decked out in props.

Despite the walking stick, he had no trouble moving around. He smirked at them as he made his way lazily out of the stall. The tattooed youngsters glanced at one another.

"Come on, old man."

"Listen, we're doin' business, so would you kindly fuck off?"

" . . . "

The last of the trio said nothing. He merely stared at the man's face, as if reminded of something.

Meanwhile, the girls were desperate to get the plastic bag they'd been promised. The one dealer pushed them back, while the other two approached the man without fear.

"This bathroom's out of order. Go somewhere else."

"My, my, kids these days are so hot-blooded! Uh-oh, am I gonna get my front teeth yanked out for saying that? Actually, you're probably too young to get that reference, aren't you?"

"The hell you talkin' about, old man?"

"Oh, it's fine if you don't know. Read more manga! You could use some bizarre adventures. Young folks like you shouldn't be old and cynical like me—you gotta get your fix of hard work, friendship, and victory!" the man cackled. He cracked his neck and held out his free hand.

" . . . ?"

The others paused. Held between his fingers was the same little plastic bag the tattooed men had been taunting the girls with earlier—only this one was totally empty.

They stared at the man in the tinted glasses, expressions frozen. He smiled and continued, "Sorry to interrupt your deal. The fellas at the door had some pretty nasty stuff in here, so I was just flushing it away. You know how it goes with toxic material—either sterilize it or flush it down the drain. I don't think it'll clog any pipes; I'm assuming it dissolves in water."

"…You asshole!"

The dealer grabbed the older man's collar with a powerful hand. He didn't even spare a thought for what might have become of those guards at the door.

"Oh, come on now, guys." There was a *brragk* sound, like a wet stick snapping. "You don't grab the collars of your superiors."

He moved slowly, smoothly—and somehow, the body of the youngster was now *spinning* through the air in a gorgeous arc. The only part of him that clashed with that pristine curve were the fingers that had been grabbing the collar, now broken and twisted.

Yet the spinning man didn't even scream. His body hurtled over and over until he landed flat on his back.

"?! *Gh——gh-kh-kh-gk!—?!—?—!*"

It was worse than having the breath knocked out of his lungs. He felt like all the oxygen and carbon dioxide in his blood vessels was being squeezed out as well.

A sensation that was impossible to distinguish between pain or numbness stole upon him, starting with the fingertips—and then he felt a shock run through his Adam's apple.

The man's walking stick was pressed against his throat. The hapless youngster passed out from the pain.

"You're lucky I'm not trained in martial arts, fella. I'd have broken more than your fingers," the older man said. The other two dealers froze in place. Time seemed to stop still.

"H-hey, what are you doing? Sell us the stuff!" the girls clamored, breaking the silence. "We have nothing to do with this dumb fight!"

One of the tattooed men bellowed, "Shut up!"

"Aaah!"

He elbowed one of the girls in the face as she tried to snatch the bag over his shoulder and then turned back to their foe.

"Now that's no good." Suddenly, the strange man was right in his face. He saw his own features, agape with shock, in the reflection from the tinted glasses.

"Wh-whoa—?!"

He tried to swing out on impulse, but there was no technique to the punch, just arm strength, and his fist hit nothing.

"Your elbows aren't meant to hit girls. You gotta be gentle with 'em."

Suddenly, the tattooed man felt a clamp on his ear, pulling him downward. "Aah...hey...you're gonna rip..."

The threat of a lost ear jolted his body's instincts, and he automatically lowered himself to keep that from happening. The man in the tinted glasses easily flipped the bruiser's feet out from under him, forcing him into a painful kiss with the bathroom floor.

"*Bwuh...fuck! Blrgh?!*"

Furious, he tried to stand, but to no avail. A foot stomped on the back of his head, breaking his nose and front teeth and sending him into the land of unconscious dreams.

His two partners' fate was sealed in stone now. The final drug dealer had terror imprinted on his features.

Now I remember.

But his fear was not caused by the violence wrought by the interloper.

Guy with a walking stick, flashy suit, tinted glasses.

He had recalled who this man was and what group he was affiliated with.

That's him...Akabayashi from the Awakusu-kai!

"W-wait, sir! I'm sorry! I'm so sorry about this!" he wailed, getting down on hands and knees to beg on the bathroom floor.

"Hey, c'mon, kid. That's nasty. Don't put your hands on the bathroom floor," Akabayashi said with a chuckle—a strange admonishment from a guy pressing a man's face into said floor. "And let me give you a piece of advice: A man shouldn't prostrate himself of his own accord. And I ain't of a mind to accept an apology that cheap. You got me?"

The prostrate young man felt the sweat on his body go cold. Through trembling lips, he mumbled, "I'm...I'm s-so sorry! I...I didn't realize you were Awakusu at first! I never would have challenged you like that..."

"Listen, you don't gotta apologize like that. If anything, *I* was the one who picked this fight with you." Akabayashi smirked. Then, for the first time, the permanent smile weakened a bit. He crouched and muttered, "If you're gonna apologize, I'm the wrong person. Right?"

"Huh...?"

Akabayashi picked up the little baggie of drugs and held it in front of the dealer's face. "This club has a number of business ties to our operation, you see. I hate to sound like a stereotype, but I'm obliged to ask: Who said you could deal this shit on our turf? Hmm? Tell the nice man."

"Er…well, I…"

"Mmm?" Akabayashi tilted his head curiously, his eyes never leaving the young man's face.

"I wasn't…umm…!"

When he caught sight of Akabayashi's eyes through the tinted lenses, he felt every muscle in his body tense up. "I—I—I d-didn't know this was Awakusu-kai territory! I s-swear, we'll pay your share f-from now on…!"

"Ha-ha-ha-ha," Akabayashi laughed mirthlessly. "Oh dear. You really don't know anything, do you?"

"H…huh…?"

"Don't you know the law, kid? Here in Japan, pills like these are illegal. But as far as I knew, you could be selling little hard candies, so I made sure to have a friend of mine examine them before I came here."

He shook his head theatrically and leaned closer to the young man. "And the thing about the places we run, like right here? We don't write the laws any *different* when it comes to dealin' this stuff. Got that?"

"Wha…?"

Are you kidding me? Why did I never hear about that?! the young man thought, stunned.

Akabayashi waggled a finger in his face and tsked. "But even if we did play that way, you don't really think we're the kind of easygoing folk who will accept an answer like, 'I'll pay your percentage off the top, sorry about that,' do you?"

"Uh…I…"

"So it's time to choose."

"Ch…choose?" the young man rasped. He realized that his breathing had been gradually getting faster and heavier. It was hard to tell what this man was saying. All he knew was that his fear of the Awakusu-kai was quickly being rivaled by that of the man before him.

He recalled the knife he had in his pocket. Should he use it or not?

Will it even work? He's a yakuza. No, I can't.

It's not like anyone knows who I am. If I kill him, I can get away. I can't. I can't escape from the yakuza. But what if they don't find out?

Dammit, why is this happening to me? It's not supposed to be like this!
Will my knife even work on this guy, anyway?
   He probably has a bigger one. Or a gun. I can't. I can't.
I can't. I can't, I can't. I can't I can't I can't I can't I can't...
A cavalcade of thoughts rushed through his brain, but not a single
one was hopeful.

"The thing is, I'm what you'd call a hypocrite. See, since I *am* in this
line of work, I do plenty of bad stuff—running gambling, setting odds,
brokering sales of crabmeat of suspect origin. But personally, I just
can't stand the drugs. That's right—it all comes down to personal likes
and dislikes. So feel free to call me a hypocrite."

Akabayashi took off the glasses and leaned closer to the young man,
who looked back into those eyes and realized something was wrong.

One of his eyes looks weird... Is it a prosthetic?

It was an odd thing to be preoccupied with at the moment. The
information was meaningless to him.

"Years ago, I was in love with a lady whose old man did her wrong
on account of these drugs. Ever since then, I've really, really hated 'em.
And the reason I'm with the Awakusu-kai now is because my likes and
dislikes can actually *mean* something."

Akabayashi chuckled dryly—and then abruptly stopped. His smile
waned. "Ah...right. You were going to choose... Which option do you
prefer?"

"Um...option?"

"For the Awakusu-kai to tie a bow on you fellas and hand you over
to the cops? Or to simply have both your arms broken?"

!!!

The youngster's breathing went so ragged it simply caught in his
throat for several seconds.

The man was going to use him as bait to strike a deal with the police.
And if he said no, his arms would be broken. Given what had just happened to his partners, he knew better than to assume it was a bluff.

"N-no...no...stop, p-please...I'm sorry! I'm sorry!" he blubbered
and rubbed his forehead against the bathroom floor again.

Akabayashi grimaced and shook his head. "For God's sake, how
does a guy with the guts to get a tattoo whimper and whine like this?
You're a disgrace to your artist."

"Th-these are just decals! W-we're not that tough, sir! I—I play it straight most of the time! It's just a little m-money on the side, they said! It wasn't my idea! I just did what they said! Please let me go! Please, please!"

"Ha-ha. In that case, you're a disgrace to whoever made that tattoo sticker... Well, damn." Akabayashi chuckled, got up, and snapped his fingers.

Suddenly, some young men in suits entered the bathroom.

"Huh? Wha—?" the dealer babbled.

"If someone's calling the shots for you, then we need to hear some more details," Akabayashi said, waving to the suits. "Take him away. Let Kazamoto handle the rest."

"Yessir." "Right away, Mr. Akabayashi."

The men in black bowed and got to work. Akabayashi rapped the floor with his stick and, in rhythm with the beat, said, "The thing is, I'm a bit squeamish when it comes to interrogation methods."

All the frightening vocabulary words had an effect. The young man finally stopped groveling and got to his feet.

I gotta run.

Even a small-time dealer wearing fake tattoos to look tough knew what would happen if he got taken to the yakuza office. He pulled out his knife and made a beeline, swinging it around threateningly.

"Hey, shithead!" "Knock it off!" Akabayashi's subordinates yelled, but the fleeing man wasn't listening. The glint of light off the silver blade as it swung about wildly elicited screams from the girls hiding in the corner of the bathroom.

"Outta my way! You wanna get stabbed?!" Fake Tat screamed, which was funny, because if he was going to hit anyone swinging the knife around like that, it was going to be a slash instead.

Akabayashi exhaled.

Not a sigh. Just a brief collecting of breath.

The young man raced straight toward him in the center of the bathroom.

"Outta—"

—my...way?

Something lightly struck the hand swinging the knife around. An object, something cylindrical, had stretched out from his blind spot and knocked the blade out of his hand.

The walking stick?

By the time he realized it, the tip of Akabayashi's cane was already out of sight again. The man's body rolled across the floor, and the end of the stick appeared from a different direction this time.

Although he held the stick like a spear with both hands, there was hardly any of its length above the left hand, so the young man's instincts told him that it wouldn't reach him. That wasn't true, of course, but the visual information his brain received resulted in that fateful illusion.

Akabayashi pushed the other end of the stick with his right hand—a very simple action—but to his victim's eyes, it looked like the point of the walking stick stretched from out of nothing.

"Whua-ffh!"

A scream of surprise and a grunt of shock both issued from his mouth simultaneously.

The tip of the cane pushed into his throat, crushing the Adam's apple. He didn't feel pain or numbness. The only thing his nerves and brain registered was something bursting.

His eyeballs instantaneously shuddered into the back of his head, and he collapsed to the floor like a rag doll.

"Okay, get him outta here," Akabayashi directed the men in suits, still smiling easily.

Once they had carried the unconscious dealer out of the bathroom, Akabayashi turned toward the end of the stalls. "Now, about you girls..."

"Eeek!"

"P-please don't..."

Until just recently, the girls had been desperate for the drugs, but the brief scene of violence and resulting conversation had made it quite clear whose presence they were in. Fear won out over desire, and they were now huddling in the corner, trembling.

"Listen, don't shiver and shake like that. Y'see, just an hour or so ago, I had to make a very pretty Russian lady sad. I'm feelin' down about upsetting the female kind right now." He chuckled, pulling out a pocket handkerchief and offering it to one of the girls. "Look at that nosebleed. Was that from the elbow? You all right? You oughta see a doctor."

"Er, uh…thank you, sir."

"You really should be quick about it. Need an escort? I mean, you're lookin' pretty pale."

"Er, uh…n-no, I'll be…fine."

The girls were shivering, trying to avoid looking into his eyes. They didn't understand what he wanted.

"P-please, help, I'll…I'll do anything…*anything!*" one of them pleaded, ready to cry.

"Aww. Oh dear. Do I really look that scary?" Akabayashi asked self-deprecatingly. He rapped the floor with the stick. "Don't you realize how lucky you are? If I were someone else, you might've been sent to an establishment for grown-up ladies, or perhaps a home-visit service, or a DVD filming studio."

This only made the girls shiver harder.

"Oh, don't get me wrong. I'm not trying to claim you owe me a favor. You heard me earlier—I'm a hypocrite, right? I'm not going to hurt you. In fact, I'm going to go the extra mile for you."

In a way, it was an even worse punishment he was proposing.

"I'm going to send you girls back home *and take it upon myself to explain to your fathers and mothers exactly what kind of medication you've been taking.*"

"…!"

"And the rest is up to you and your families. See? You'll be in a hospital no matter what."

"Oh, and…depending on circumstances, there might be some business between your families and *us.*"

♂♀

Several minutes later, in a taxi

Akabayashi gave his subordinates their orders and left the club alone. Then he got into a cab, muttering to himself.

"Always leaves a bad aftertaste when you make a girl cry."

The driver overheard this and decided to meddle. "What's that? Have a fight with your lady?"

"Let's call it that. No punches or anything, but she was quite sad about the whole thing," Akabayashi said, shaking his head.

The elderly driver laughed and scolded, "Shouldn't do that. You gotta be gentle with women."

"That's what I've been saying."

A few minutes later, Akabayashi's cell phone rang. It played the latest hit from the singer Ruri Hijiribe.

"Oh, sir! What do you know, it's your lady friend!"

"Ha-ha-ha...if only," Akabayashi replied, indulging the driver.

He hit the accept button. "Hello? It's your buddy."

"Don't answer the phone like a creep. It's me," said the caller— Akabayashi's fellow Awakusu-kai lieutenant, Aozaki.

He'd been involved with the Russian trouble just a few hours ago, so Akabayashi assumed the call was related. "What is it, Aozaki? Something happen with our Russian guest?"

"No, it's not that. You hear about the young miss?"

"You mean how Heiwajima and the Black Rider helped her? I'm guessin' that Mikiya's probably giving her a scolding for running away from home and feelin' relieved on the inside."

The "young miss" was Akane Awakusu, the daughter of Mikiya Awakusu, underboss of the Awakusu-kai, and furthermore, she was granddaughter of Dougen Awakusu, the head of the organization. She'd run away from home for the past few days and wound up in quite a bit of trouble, including being kidnapped by the Russians in question. It was only this evening that they got word she was safe again.

"No...not quite. Apparently, she's been acting odd," Aozaki answered.

"Odd?"

"Well...this is all secondhand, so I don't know for sure, and it ain't really my business to care. But you've known her pretty well since she was a little girl, yeah?"

"I suppose. I'll ask Mikiya about it tomorrow... Funny that *you* should be concerned, though. I thought you hated Mikiya," Akabayashi teased.

"Don't give me that shit," Aozaki growled through the speaker.

"Yeah, I'm not fully on board with Mikiya, but Miss Akane is the old man's granddaughter. If anything happens to her, we go to war. Of course I'm concerned."

"But isn't that what you want, Aozaki?"

"...I said, don't give me that shit, you bungling clown," Aozaki snorted, clicking his tongue, and hung up.

Akabayashi looked down at his phone, shaking his head.

At that moment, the driver asked, "Is this a good spot for you, sir?"

"Uh, sure. Just up at that corner."

"You got it."

Compared with earlier, the driver's smile was forced and unnatural. He'd heard enough from that call to recognize Akabayashi's occupation.

"Sorry I couldn't give you a longer trip fare. Here, keep the change for your trouble."

"Oh! Oh no, sir! I couldn't take this whole bill!"

"Trust me, it's fine," Akabayashi insisted, shoving the ten-thousand-yen bill into the driver's hand. He exited the taxi, cracked his neck, and looked up at the neon-lit night sky of the big city.

"...Things've been strange lately."

The Black Rider.

The return of the slasher.

The rise of the Dollars.

Trouble with Ruri Hijiribe.

Jinnai Yodogiri.

And now this incident with the Russians and Akane.

"Well, there's always been troubles in any city," he muttered to himself, then headed for the apartment where he spent his nights.

But even still, things've been strange. It's like the light and the dark side of town are bleeding together. Maybe those folks on the bright side are having trouble keeping to their own.

He looked back up at the sky, realizing that it was pointless to wonder. The light of the town and the dark of the night mingled, hiding the stars behind the muddled haze.

Akabayashi gazed at the ambiguity and mumbled, "I don't like that sky."

*   *   *

"Bright or dark—make up your damn mind."

♂♀

Six years ago

The man who had dyed himself with the color of violence would hurt others again today.

He felt a glow of ecstasy every time he saw the scars he inflicted on someone else.

That scar is me.

The blood they shed, the red of their exposed flesh, the sound of their bones breaking—these are the things that make me as a person.

It was less a statement of pride or ideals than a shallow fantasy, a daydream.

He would fall apart unless he hurt someone.

This self-created illusion acted as a wicked mold of his instincts.

In this city, the scars he left on others were his footprints.

With each act of violence, his glory grew and so did his intoxication.

With no fatigue and no reflection upon the past, as if it were his reason for living.

Change came to him at last when he took on a certain job.

The owner of a certain business owed a debt, and the man's organization took it on.

It wasn't quite in the midst of the busy shopping district, but it was still land in the capital.

So the job was quite simple: Seize the land as collateral for the debt.

But things went awry. Somehow, the owner got the money and paid back what he owed.

A simple story of bad luck, if it had ended right there.

But the business owner, seemingly mad, demanded money from the organization.

He tried to blackmail them, to threaten them with legal trouble for an illegal collection scheme.

The owner's mind was probably not on sound footing at that point.

They decided that he could not be reasoned with and gave the man a new job.

Put the hurt on him.

Nice and clean. Nice and simple.

The owner had a family, too, so if necessary, the man was allowed to involve them.

Of course, it couldn't look like the work of the man's organization, so he had to make it appear as a robbery and rough them up in a nonfatal way.

On the night of the new moon, the man put on a ski mask and headed for the business in question.

It was an antique shop in Ikebukuro.

The name: Sonohara-dou.

♂♀

May 5, morning, home of Mikiya Awakusu

The residence of Mikiya Awakusu, *waka-gashira* underboss of the Awakusu-kai, was virtually indistinguishable from any of the other homes in the distant suburbs of Ikebukuro and gave no indication that its occupants were anything but normal.

On the contrary, it was the kind of house so pristine that the cynical might be prompted to claim, "The only people who would live in a house so nice are the ones who do dirty deeds for dirty money." In short, it was just a very fancy house.

Once inside the home, the tottering steps of a young girl rushed to greet him.

"Mr. Akabayashi!"

"Ahh, young miss. It's nice to see you again."

In fact, it had been years since he'd popped his head in. In the past, he'd often come by to visit and spend time with the girl, but now that Akane was getting on with school, he had bowed out and kept his distance, respecting Mikiya's wish to keep the family business a secret from her.

Ultimately, that concerted effort had fallen through, and she had learned the truth of what her father did for a living. From what Akabayashi heard, it was the reason she ran away from home, but thankfully, she was back safe and sound now.

"…I heard you wanted to see me, miss?"

"Yeah!" she said, nodding vigorously. She seemed to be bursting with lively cheer, but that seemed unnatural for one who had been kidnapped just a day ago.

Normally, he would have gotten the details of the incident from Mikiya at the office. Instead, it was Mikiya who had approached *him*.

"My daughter wants to talk to you. Will you come to the house with me?"

"Me? What for?"

"I wish I knew, but she won't tell me."

Acting odd indeed, he'd thought, recalling the phone conversation with Aozaki the night before. Still, Akabayashi wrapped up his afternoon business early and headed off to see Akane.

Once the little girl saw him in person, she reached over to tug his sleeve, eyes sparkling. "I have something I want to talk about in private, Mr. Akabayashi. Can you come to my room?"

"Now, Akane," Mikiya warned, but the man waved him off.

"Oh, it's fine, Director. I don't mind."

He started off to follow the girl, but this time it was Mikiya who pulled on his sleeve.

"I trust I don't need to warn you not to fill her head with nonsense?"

"I know, sir."

"And keep your hands to yourself."

"…Mikiya, do you actually know how old your daughter is?" Akabayashi snorted, shaking his head.

"Ah. Y-yes, of course, sorry. I thought maybe you had intentions of…"

"No, I didn't. Not in the least, Mikiya."

"You're right… I'm sorry. It's just, I remember when you were looking after some girl somewhere a few years back. I thought maybe your tastes ran… No, never mind. Ignore me. You weren't messing around with that kid, either."

"No, it's fine. I get it—I don't have a wife or even a woman. Some folks whisper that I'm not a ladies' man in the first place. Ha-ha," Akabayashi chuckled easily and headed for Akane's room without sign of offense.

When he walked through her door, Akane greeted him with a serious expression on her face. "Listen...I want you to keep this a secret from my parents."

"Of course, I get it," he said with a smile, crouching down to put her at ease.

She started off innocently enough. "Umm, so...uhh..."

But then it got much worse.

"How can I...get good at killing people?"

Her eyes were innocent, pure, and so serious.

Well, I'll be damned, Akabayashi thought, feeling a rare cold sweat break out on his skin.

He sighed—but never let that easy, lazy grin leave his lips.

This is a hell of a lot more than "acting odd."

♂♀

Thirty minutes later, in a car

"...So what was it that Akane asked about? She said 'talk to you later,' right at the end. Are you going to see her again today?"

"Oh, it was just a bit of small talk. And a secret, too."

They were in the backseat of a luxury car on the way to the Awakusu-kai office. Akabayashi smirked carelessly as usual from the seat next to Mikiya's.

"...Akabayashi."

"Really, it was nothing major. Maybe what happened yesterday gave her some ideas? She said she wants to get stronger. I happen to know someone who runs a dojo—more like a sports gym—that teaches women and children self-defense in addition to the usual stuff. I said I'd take her there this afternoon."

"Oh...I see. Why would she ask you, though?"

"Ha-ha, well, that's the funny part." Akabayashi chuckled, pulling out his cell phone.

"What are you doing...?"

"Do you know how the young miss learned about our work?"

"...No."

"This thing here." He showed Mikiya his phone screen, which was displaying a webpage.

"Ahh...I recognize that."

It was an Internet encyclopedia—*Fuguruma Youki*.

The site was a freely editable online encyclopedia in the mold of *Wikipedia*, where users congregated to add their own information and build a massive database. While much of the information was faulty or based on rumors and lies, these things could be corrected by other users or even the people featured in the articles themselves.

"I had the younger guys correct a lot of the particularly sensitive bits."

The site's article on the Awakusu-kai had all kinds of detailed information on their operation—even down to the names of principal members—right there in the open for anyone to read. Mikiya saw his name on the phone screen and scowled.

"So she could have seen it on her phone? Convenience is making our job harder now."

"This is what happens when you give a kid an online-accessible phone without thinking. But the cat's out of the bag now, and that ain't my problem." Akabayashi chuckled.

Mikiya glared at him, then down at the phone again, where he saw his underling's name on the article as well. It featured simple profiles of the group members, and his read, "A capable fighter with many legends under his belt. Along with Aozaki, they are known as the Red Ogre and Blue Ogre of the Awakusu-kai, respectively."

"Look at how they puff us up. Basically, the young miss read this nonsense, and since she knew me from her childhood, she decided to ask me for self-defense help."

If Akabayashi wore a permanent, lopsided grin, Mikiya's face was equally frozen in a frightening scowl. "Well...better you than Aozaki. But I would have hoped that Akane would talk to me or her mother first."

"Ha-ha, she probably just doesn't want to make you folks worry more than she already has. She's a good daughter."

"My daughter trying to keep me from worrying is the most concerning thing I can fret over. So...I assume this dojo or sports gym or whatever is a trustworthy place?"

"Oh yes. It's a regular old place, no yakuza operation. It's the one over near Zoshigaya Cemetery. You know that German fighter, Traugott Geissendorfer? It's kind of a worldwide chain that teaches his dojo style..."

The conversation continued on in this manner.

At this point, Akabayashi was not outright lying, but he also wasn't telling the entire story. And for his part, he knew that Akane hadn't told him everything, either. He chose not to pry into it—but the girl had clearly been partially *broken* by someone.

Resigned, Akabayashi decided that what Akane needed right now was to interact with more people, those who wouldn't treat her like something exotic and special. The best option for that was the dojo.

There will be plenty of other girls there, too.

He mulled over the benefits of asking Akane for more information later in the afternoon versus keeping his distance and observing her more.

*   *   *

Next to him, stone-faced, Mikiya decided to broach a completely different topic. "You cracked down on some kids pushing last night, didn't you?"

"Ah, that? I put Kazamoto in charge of it."

"...Well, it's turned into a bit of a thing."

"Pardon?"

Despite all the ups and downs of what happened with his daughter, Mikiya's frank, flat delivery betrayed no emotion. "I assumed they had to be working under some group or other...but nothing. They say it's just a regular *college club*."

"Club?"

"They're students at Raira College... Just normal students by most accounts, but those ones you pulverized all had the same stickers on their necks, right? The fake tattoos."

"That's right, they did," Akabayashi said, recalling the young men from the previous night. He'd nearly forgotten the details already.

They had flashy tattoos visible around their throats and collarbones, but even they admitted that the marks were just removable decals.

"Raira College is actually a fairly prestigious school. Just goes to show, there are idiots to be found anywhere."

"I see. So I guess they just cultivated and mixed those pills themselves? Y'know, there's something to be said for young entrepreneurship." Akabayashi chuckled, shaking his head.

Mikiya noticed that the smile did not extend to his companion's eyes and glanced at the cell phone again. "Well, they're certainly crafty. Everyone in their operation from the dealers on up communicate only through phones. They change numbers regularly, so they must be using burners."

Burners were phones registered under falsified names designed to be used for short periods of time. It was easy enough to pay a large number of people a small amount of money (or a bit of debt relief) to sign up for a phone and then collect the phones for anonymous use. Once the cellular contract ran out or the police got involved, the phones were unusable, so you just switched to the next disposable phone. It was a favored tactic for scam artists and others outside the law.

As a matter of fact, Mikiya and the Awakusu found burners to be handy tools at times, too. "Kazamoto said he'd run the numbers of the phones past his burner dealer, but it's not clear if we'll be able to track down whoever's at the center of this operation. Apparently, they're all college students, though…"

Mikiya tsked his tongue, his expression still flat. "It's an ugly time to be alive. Normal-lookin' kids, using the Internet or whatever to get into *our* side of the business? People talk about the yakuza blending in with regular professionals—but these kids are just straight-up normal."

"Good point. If those guys yesterday didn't have the fake tattoos, they'd just look like ordinary fellas who happened to be well-built."

"…By the way, you know about a group of kids called the Dollars?"

"Where's this comin' from?" Akabayashi asked, not bothering to mention or deny his registration as a member of that very group.

"Well, the kids who Kazamoto 'questioned' yesterday told us a whole bunch of stuff…but one of the things they mentioned was that there was some kind of upper organization that they only talked to on the phone…"

"Apparently, they were founded after the Dollars' model—only this group just sells drugs online."

♂♀

The same moment, Awakusu-kai headquarters

The Awakusu-kai was an organized crime operation, or what the rest of society termed a "violence group." It was a large group, one of the midsized members of the Medei-gumi Syndicate. No one outside of the gang had a firm grasp on their total number, but the name itself carried quite a bit of clout within Ikebukuro.

In the depths of the office building that the group used as a headquarters, a spare room held an overbearing atmosphere, as a person spoke in a gravelly voice.

"Ahh. There is no problem with that matter."

The timbre of the voice marked him as a significantly elderly man. But there was powerful strength to it, as well as a solid menace, like a looming craggy mountain.

"We have no intention of souring our relationship with you. However, we cannot handle the matter ourselves, you understand. With reconciliation with the Asuki-gumi at hand, it would not do to have rumors that we are killing our own. If he screwed up, that would be one thing, but this is entirely your own request."

There was no answering voice from within the room; he was apparently speaking on the phone.

"But...I can promise you that however you wish to settle things with him, the Awakusu-kai will not take action. If he should meet an unfortunate accident or turn up missing, that would not weaken our position with the Asuki-gumi."

He spoke in clear, polite language, neither debasing himself nor patronizing his conversation partner. It was clinical and businesslike, with no hint of personal emotion.

"On the other hand, you will not harm anyone else of ours. If anyone *else*, be it member of our organization or their relatives, is brought into this—there will be a reckoning."

After this there were a few more statements, and the speaker ended his call. A wrinkled hand set down the receiver gingerly, as if licking at the air.

During the call, he had been perfectly composed and utterly in control, but his next words were a lament. "Even after decades...I just can't get used to this phone thing."

Hanging lanterns and a little shrine altar decorated the space, making it the only room in the place, decked out as it was like some kind of securities office, that looked like the chamber of a traditional yakuza.

Sitting in the back of this head honcho's office was the speaker, sunk deep into a rich leather chair. It creaked, releasing some of the suffocating tension in the room. He leaned back behind his desk—which was simple in design but clearly built of very fine wood—and gave a toothy grin.

"Funny thing is, most of my teeth are fake by now. Got a couple of bolts jammed into my pelvis. Wouldn't that make me a— What's the thing from the movies? Cyborg? A robocop? And somehow I don't know my way around a machine. God musta made some mistake with me."

He rubbed the silent phone receiver and addressed the large man standing near the door. "What about you, Aozaki? You like phones?"

Aozaki and the old man were the only ones in the room. He bowed his head and rumbled, "If you want me to, boss, I'll destroy my own cell phone in a snap."

It sounded like a joke, but the tone of voice indicated otherwise. The old man, Dougen Awakusu, just chuckled and shook his head.

"If you don't call me 'Chairman,' you'll get an earful from our director and Shiki, too."

Dougen was in his early sixties, if appearance was any judge. His actual age was a mystery, but the full white beard did a good job of projecting maturity. It was well-kept, so he looked more like Santa Claus than some ragged old hermit from a fairy tale.

The other man, one of the most combative and aggressive of the Awakusu officers, said politely, "There's no one around to hear me, boss. So was that call about the you-know-what?"

"Hmm? Ahh yes. Is that what you're here to talk about, too?"

"Indeed. I'm surprised that those remnants are still going after him— and even more surprised that they actually called you directly, boss. Say the word, and I'll have them wiped out within a day," Aozaki said.

His words were rough, but his deference to the boss was unmistakable. He was an overbearing man by nature, and he often slighted Mikiya, the actual heir to the group—but he had nothing but deep respect for the Awakusu boss before him.

"Ha-ha, I'm sure you could. You're not the Blue Ogre of Awakusu for nothing."

"Don't mention that, please. It makes it sound like I'm just great pals with that Red Ogre guy."

"What's the harm in that? You know you respect Akabayashi's skill."

"Oh, he's trustworthy in a fight, that's for sure, but it means nothing against a whole organization. He might have that little group of pet bikers under his wing, but the man's not suited for working with a team."

Aozaki paused, squinted up at the ceiling.

"Which is probably why *stuff like this* comes up."

Dougen Awakusu cackled dryly and said, "Perhaps. Those remnants want nothing more than to kill Akabayashi. Nothing else matters to them."

"What group are they affiliated with now?"

"You promised to snuff them out in a day without knowing the answer to that question? Well...I suppose I should have expected that from you."

Dougen leaned forward off the back of the chair, resting his elbows on the desk. He tapped the surface with his index finger and smiled cruelly. "Apparently, a number of them got out of jail recently and decided to start their own group. It operates under the guise of a small realty office."

"They never learn."

"Can you blame them? They've still got their suspicions," Dougen said, stroking his beard with an eager smile.

"They still think it was Akabayashi who killed their old boss."

♂♀

There was a rumor about Akabayashi.

While he was an important officer with the Awakusu-kai, he hadn't come up through the organization. In fact, he had originally been a muscle man for a rival group that had fought with the Awakusu for territory in Ikebukuro.

He wasn't really just a disposable muscle man used for suicide missions, but a highly prized all-around weapon for the group. His presence there was invaluable...

But the group did not last.

The *kumicho*—the boss of the group—was murdered.

At the same time, the police discovered a large drug-smuggling operation the group was running and arrested most of them. It was essentially disbanded.

But Akabayashi, one of the most notable of its members, was absent from the major arrest. And he had been the bodyguard with the *kumicho* when the murder happened.

These two facts were enough to plant suspicion in the minds of the men who got caught. Perhaps he had killed the boss and ratted them out to the cops.

Their suspicions festered and grew, but no evidence supported them.

And now, Akabayashi was a principal member of the Awakusu-kai, their former rivals. Regardless of suspicions of murder, this was more than enough to earn the rancor of his former comrades.

But then the Awakusu-kai were brought under the umbrella of the Medei-gumi, and the remnants of that now-rival gang were totally powerless to do anything about the matter.

And now, the man in question was known as the Red Ogre of Awakusu. However, most of the fame behind that moniker stemmed from his past exploits; since joining the Awakusu, he had been a valuable member but was seen as a relative moderate among the muscle flexers.

And of course, there were those like Shiki, who saw Akabayashi's aloof attitude as a mask to hide his true nature and stayed cautious of the man.

♂♀

"Most of the ones who handled the drugs are still locked up, but for those who did manage to get out early, I bet they were sure Akabayashi did it, once they found out he's with us now."

"Normally, when you kill your own, you don't last long in our world. Where there's smoke, you gotta assume there's fire…and yet you brought him aboard, boss."

"I suppose I like to go against the grain. And I wasn't going to be shy about a few rumors when there was good money to be made. Somehow, he really gets around with the younger folks." Dougen cackled.

"But you just cut down that money tree on the phone right now," Aozaki cautioned.

"Perhaps I did."

"Let us settle our score with Akabayashi."

That was the request the brand-new group had been making of Dougen recently.

They were former rivals, fresh out of prison. Normally, this matter would have been ignored, but from the very start, these fellows seemed suicidally desperate.

"We don't intend to start anything with you. But none of us can go to our deaths knowing that we haven't avenged our boss. If you cover for him, we're prepared to go out in a blaze of glory."

Ultimately, Dougen ended up giving them his answer, minutes ago: "If you make it unrelated to our group, through accident or disappearance, we will not retaliate."

This wasn't out of some yakuza tradition of honor or recognizing a wrong that ought to be made right. It wasn't out of respect for their desperate gamble to avenge their slain leader.

To Dougen, it was sheer practicality: Starting a war now would make the Medei-gumi look bad and lower their standing before making peace with the Asuki-gumi.

On top of that, men fresh out of prison would naturally be under police scrutiny. Starting trouble with a desperate gang was a risk for very little reward—even if they could be crushed "in a day," as Aozaki promised.

They were no fools. They were men of the night, responsible for building the darkness of Ikebukuro.

"You see, I can't betray my men...but I can abandon them."

♂♀

Six years ago, Tokyo, near Sonohara-dou

It was supposed to be like any other night.

The job was simple: Act like a robber and rough up a store owner.

He had given up a tender conscience long ago. He never even thought about guilt anymore.

What possible threat could the owner of an antique curio shop pose? The man's arrogance was a symbol of his violence.

He had little interest in money or women. But he didn't glorify poverty, and he wasn't attracted to men. He just loved being a conduit for violence.

"If necessary, involve the wife and kid," they'd told him, but he wasn't particularly interested in doing that. He just wanted to rough up the owner and be done with it. He'd never been violent against women and children, but it wasn't out of some sense of kindness or chivalry—he just found no interest in doing so, because it wasn't worth bragging about.

He didn't know how he started learning how to fight. What was more important was that he had honed his skill through constant combat and experience.

He had no interest in humans themselves—they were vivid targets for exhibiting violence, but little else. His fist was clenched today for the sole purpose of displaying his strength, to create new scars that would speak of his existence.

But as he approached Sonohara-dou, he noticed a figure standing in the street. He had chosen a moonless night, so the only light to illuminate the person was the flickering streetlamps. He couldn't really tell who it was.

"Hey…who are you?"

He couldn't just ignore them and continue on his way.
There was a long silver object in the figure's hand—a katana.

"…A shock trooper sent to eliminate me? If you think havin' a sword will give you the edge, you're gonna learn a real painful lesson," the man threatened, cracking his neck aggressively.

Normally, he would seize the advantage by throwing something before talking, but on this day, he didn't. Something about the figure, something eerie, chilled his instincts.

Once he was within ten steps of the katana's range—

The blade flickered, like a heat haze in midsummer.

That ripple in the darkness threw off his sense of distance. It felt as if the figure had approached five steps within a single flicker of the streetlight.

But in fact, there was another part of the scene he felt closing the distance.

The sword...stretched...?!

The blade should have been an ordinary length for a katana, but in the span of that brief moment, it changed shape, stretching to nearly double the length.

The man knew from experience that while a solid thrust or *iai* drawing of a blade could create the illusion of shifting distance, this was not one of those cases.

The reason he couldn't understand it was because the truth was that *the blade really did stretch.*

The streetlight flickered on again, and he was able to see the figure clearly.

A woman?!

It was a woman wearing indoor clothing—her eyes glowing red like the light on a police car.
Wait, is that who they talk about...?
Like two red moons shining from her eye sockets.
Gleaming. Blazing.
The slasher...

The next time the light flickered on, his mind reached further depths of confusion. Somehow there was another katana stretching for him, but from where her shoulder met her neck, rather than her hand. The tip reached out to him, desperate to pierce his skin.
—!
He leaped sideways on reflex, evading the two oncoming blades by just the slimmest of margins. When he recovered his stance and turned back, ready to fight, his body froze.
What is this?
Blades.
What am I looking at?
Not just from her shoulder.
What the hell is this?
The silver of the blade was protruding from her limbs, her back, her stomach—even the ends of her long hair. It wasn't chaotic growth

like wild mushrooms, but functional and methodical, sprouting from locations like her elbows, such that the blades were like bits of body armor.

What am I looking at?

A mechanical puppet, a robot bristling with blades.

Those red glowing eyes had to be made with light bulbs, he imagined. It was an utterly nonsensical image, but the thing was there. Right in front of him.

Is this...real life?

It was a monster. The slasher was a monster.

A red-eyed monster sprouting katana blades wherever it wanted on its body, performing impossible feats.

He didn't know this monster's name.

"Dammit..."

He was unfamiliar with Saika, the cursed blade that loved humanity.

"What the hell are you, dammit?!"

There was no reply. The monster clutched in the red-eyed woman's hand spurred its wielder's body onward into a direct leap toward the paralyzed man. It was the jump of a female lead in a romance movie, leaping into the arms of the man she loved.

But this sword's lips did not caress the man's mouth or his cheek.

He managed to break out of his emergency paralysis and tried to move out of the way.

But the tip of the sword stretched out even farther...

And *split* his right eye, directly down the middle.

♂♀

Present day, Tokyo, empty room

There was an air of abnormality shrouding the shop.

It was an empty building that combined a storefront and living space under one roof, plopped down in the midst of an ordinary residential area far from the station and shopping district.

There was a sign out front reading SONOHARA-DOU, but the letters were faded and missing so that it was nearly impossible to make out any longer. All the furnishings that identified it as an old antique shop were still there, but the display cases visible from the outside were full of nothing but piled-up dust.

It was obvious at first sight that the building was abandoned, though the details of the empty display cases and oddly patterned pillars gave the place a type of presence that went past strange and right into creepy.

A man stood in front of it, unbothered by this aura, giving the building a wistful look.

"Five years, and this place still hasn't sold. Figures."

After dropping Akane off at his acquaintance's gym, Akabayashi came to visit this abandoned store by himself. He wasn't doing anything in particular—just staring at the place through his tinted glasses—when he heard a faint voice nearby.

"...Mr....Akabayashi?"

"Hmm?" He spun around and saw a girl standing there. She looked shy and quiet and wore the Raira Academy uniform, along with a pair of glasses. She'd probably been watching him approach with trepidation before calling out, but the gangster broke into a grin.

"...Ohh! Is that you, Anri? You're so much taller now. How long has it been...? Two years?"

"Yes, it's nice to see you again... What brings you here?" Anri asked, bowing. She didn't seem afraid of the man.

"Oh, I was just in the area. What's with the uniform? Shouldn't you be on break today?"

"I had to show up at school for the class representatives' meeting... I was just getting home now."

"Gotcha. Must be hard having to go to school during your vacation," Akabayashi offered with a breezy smile.

"Umm...I really should thank you for what you did."

"You know, you say that every time we meet, but you really don't need to. I'm the one who owes a debt to...to your mother."

"But...if you hadn't helped me find a new apartment back then, who knows what might have happened to me...? I lost my father and mother and had to leave the house..."

She put on a rare, gentle smile, one of pure gratitude.

Anri Sonohara lost her parents years ago in an incident.

She wound up passed around among her relatives, a time of great upheaval—and ultimately, they sold off many of the remaining Sonohara-dou items to put together a fund that would pay for her living costs until she was an adult.

The person who helped deal with this inheritance fund was a man named Akabayashi, who came to pay his respects at her parents' funeral. Later, when she decided to move out on her own and save her relatives the trouble, Akabayashi was there to help arrange an apartment for her. He claimed that he owed her parents a favor and helped her with a number of very important things, all for free. She felt nothing but gratitude toward him.

She bowed, over and over, so Akabayashi scratched his head uncomfortably and changed the topic.

"So, uh, is that the Raira uniform? You're in high school already, then. Wait...second year?"

"Yes, that's right..."

She bowed yet again, and Akabayashi scratched at his cheek this time.

Suddenly, he recalled things Mikiya had said in the car earlier in the day:

"I don't know if it's like a game to them or what, but even in this college club, the guys at the top are bad news. They believe they're totally safe from trouble, even against the real thing like us... They had beef with another gang in the past, and the fellows in that group got attacked.

"You need to be careful. Don't hang around with Akane too much. I'll set it up so that someone else goes to the dojo tonight to get her.

"In any case, this is very abrupt stuff, so while I'll spare some protection for Akane, I don't have the extra leeway to guard you, too. You'll have to fend for yourself."

Something about what Mikiya said snagged in Akabayashi's head. He said to Anri, "I'm curious—I have a question about school fads for you."

"Y-yes…? Well…I'm really not that up on fads, either…"

"It's fine. I'll take whatever you can tell me," he said and decided to bring up the name, figuring she wouldn't know. "Anri, have you ever heard the name Dollars at school?"

Her breath briefly caught in her throat. He noticed the change and asked, "You know something, then?"

"N-no…just…that I've heard a friend talk about it… But I don't know any details."

"…"

It was painfully obvious that she was lying. Akabayashi wasn't going to rake her over the coals for it, but he also wanted more information.

"Ah, I see," he said and patted her on the shoulder with a smile. "They're dangerous folks I hear, so steer clear of them. And if anything happens, you let me know at once."

"Oh no… I couldn't impose on you any further…"

"No, I insist. You know I got a lotta clout around here, right? So call on me for anything. You got a problem? Just call that number I gave you. On the other hand…since I'm so well-known, there are folks who don't like me. So if you happen to see me around town and don't have anything to ask, feel free to ignore me."

"Uhh…"

Perhaps she didn't realize what he did for a living; in which case, the girl probably thought he was acting rather strange. Akabayashi gave her his usual tilted grin and was about to say something to put her at ease—

When a third party interrupted him.

"Is that you, Sonohara?" said the voice. He spun around to see a young man.

"Oh...Yagiri," said Anri. It was Seiji Yagiri, the boyfriend of her best friend, Mika Harima.

The newcomer glanced around the area. "Wait, so...does that mean you're done with whatever you were doing with Mika?"

"Huh...?"

She was confused, and now, so was he.

Recognizing that the two were friends, Akabayashi turned his back and waved to her. "Well, I'll just be going now. You take care of yourself, hear?"

"Oh...yes! Of course! Thank you!" she replied, still bobbing up and down, until Akabayashi left the vicinity of Sonohara-dou.

"So who was that?" Seiji asked.

She smiled and said, "That was Mr. Akabayashi. He knew my mother...and he's done a lot to help me."

"What does he do?"

"Umm...I heard he delivers fresh crabs or runs a café or something... I think he does all kinds of stuff."

"Huh... Seems like a strange guy..."

Seiji was still curious about Akabayashi, but then he came to his senses and returned to the topic on his mind.

"Oh, right. So are you saying you *weren't* the person who called Mika earlier?"

"What...?"

Within seconds, Seiji Yagiri realized the truth and headed in a rush for a certain pharmaceutical company's warehouse lot.

But that's another story.

♂♀

Six years ago

A shock ran through the skin around his right eye.

He could feel that much.

But whatever happened after that was a mystery.

*　　*　　*

A voice.

"I love you."

A voice, an overwhelming voice that drowned out everything else, commanded his brain.

It was coming from around his eye, where he just felt the shock.

Oh, I see.

Understanding was instantaneous.

That katana hit my right eye...

And it was as if the eye itself was screaming in pain.

The voice raced from his eye through the rest of him, shredding his nerves, his bones, his muscle, his brain.

It was an unstoppable flood of words that threatened to wash his mind away. It was as if they had form, a solidity like lead that rocketed around inside his body.

For the first time in his life, he felt fear. He felt his mind and flesh being devoured from the inside out.

The voice speaking of "love" might erase him entirely. It might alter him, re-create him as something else.

The man who lived through nothing but violence now felt a bizarre, foreign fear.

However—amid his fear, he felt a different impulse rising within him.

This, too, was an overwhelming urge that he had never experienced before.

Hey... What the hell is this? Why now? What am I thinking?

But all the while, the voice grew, increasing its pressure.

It grew to hold its own will, flooding his heart with words of love and

                                                                                    and

                                                          and

                                              love

                                          love

                                    was all

                              ve, love, love, lo

                        ause of love." "So mu

                  ust love people." "Don't be ridicu

            "Don't talk about who you love, that just

      o, no, no! I love all, all, all of humanity equally

                              "Shut up for a second."

What do I love? Don't be ridiculous! It's everything

      love blood splatter." "I love hard bone." "It's love." "Nice

            so I forgive you." "So you can forgive me, too, okay" "I
            won't

                  all of this." "Ah!" "The slice of meat during the
                  moment of ecstasy

            I just love the soft and yet hard muscle that rips right
            apart!" "And there's

      that hard bone, so smooth and supple, weak yet sharp, tough
      and cracking!" "Love

trembling and soft and silky and squishy sticking and sticking
and sticking tight together

as voices echo with cries of love, yes? I'm so jealous I wish I had
words of love to speak but I

don't so I want you to love me instead I want to be filled but yes oh
yes but oh yes I'm so jealous even dying can be a form of love lust is a
powerful form of love but no you can't try to narrow love to a definition that's blasphemy against the heart there is no definition of love all
that you need are those simple words I love you I love you I love you I
love you

"Shut up."

I love...lo...? ...ve? ...love...love...love...love?

"I said, shut the fuck up, stupid eye!"

The echoing words of love inside of him abruptly stopped.

At the same time, there was a click, a snapping sound from around his right eye.

The first was merely a mental sound; the second was a physical process in his retina.

"...!"

It was actually the slasher who was most surprised by this change.

He had reached up to the eye that was just cut—*and gouged it out with his own hand.*

Then he crushed it in his palm and stood boldly before the slasher. The fear from moments ago was gone now, and in what light could be gleaned from the now-stabilizing streetlight overhead, his remaining eye glared fiercely.

An ordinary person might have yelped in the face of that glare. But the slasher chose to speak to him instead.

"...You're really something."

"..."

"I've never seen someone escape from this girl's voice before. Saika was so shocked that she drew back inside of me. Maybe she's feeling like she just got dumped," the woman said, her voice soothing, perhaps even relieved.

It certainly didn't sound like the voice of a mad, indiscriminate attacker. She walked closer to him. The countless blades were gone from her skin, leaving only the one katana in her hands, now its ordinary length.

"I'm happy... I thought no one would ever try to stop her..."

Large tears spilled from her glowing red eyes. The droplets caught that red light, making it look as though blood was dripping from her tear ducts.

"Are you going...to finish me at last?" she asked. It sounded like a request to die.

He shook his head. "No...sorry. I have no idea what you're talking about."

Then he started striding forward, no fear of her deadly sword. "But...I had something I wanted to tell you. I had to shut up that annoying noise first—that's all."

Already he was within the katana's range. But she did not slice at him.

"What's your name?"

"..."

"Actually, never mind. I don't need your name."

Then he was close enough to reach out and touch her. He came to a stop there.

And as the red-eyed woman watched in surprise and confusion, he spoke.

—Spoke the words brought by that *other* impulse within him, spoke his mind in a way he had never done before.

"...*I'm in love with you.*"

"...Huh?" she said, red eyes wide.

Those simple words represented his entire life being staked on a gamble.

He had built himself through the scars he'd inflicted on others. And now the words tumbled out of him as if he were trying to eject all those ugly red marks at once.

"For the first time in my life, I believed a woman was beautiful. I wanted to hug and squeeze one."

"..."

"I don't care if you're human, or a monster, or even some kind of Buddhist goddess. All that matters is that I love you as a *woman*," he said, his speech getting gradually faster as his self-control failed to hide his agitation. "Even I know that this is crazy to say, comin' right after we just met, and you sliced my damn eyeball...but I ain't pretending it's based on logic. Please—marry me!"

The entire scene had only taken a few minutes. She was a monster. He just lost the sight of one of his eyes forever. Anyone would assume that his sanity had buckled under the extreme circumstances.

But the man's brain was operating quite normally, successfully withstanding the pain and loss of that eyeball. It was much later that he realized that not only was it "love at first sight," it was also "love at single sight."

A person he'd only ever identified as a target to be hurt—a "weak, fragile" woman—had turned out to be a presence every bit his equal, completely capable of killing him.

The ghostliness of those glowing red eyes, the feminine figure, the flowing black hair melting into the darkness of night—all these things melded together in womanly beauty and enchanted his heart.

He'd never professed love before.

This innocence, his first ever feelings of romance, got under the cracks of his protective pride—his violence—and shot it someplace far, far away.

But that very first confession ended in failure.

"...Thank you. I'm very flattered that you said you love me, even like this," she chuckled with a hint of sadness. "But I'm afraid I can't return the feeling."

She shook her head and spoke the only two words that could cut him deeper than her katana already had: "I'm married."

"...!"

"I still love my husband and daughter. So I can't reciprocate your sentiment."

The sheer finality of that statement made his knees quake. Whether through sadness, anger, embarrassment, or the strange beauty of her rejection, he promptly slapped his cheeks with both hands. The blood drooling from his mutilated eye socket stained his hand even further. Intense pain shot through his face.

But he held fast without yelling, silencing the trembling in his knees through willpower alone.

"I see... That's too bad. But...can I at least get your name?"

"..."

"Don't worry. I'm not going to bother your husband or daughter."

She seemed hesitant, but something in his gaze eventually convinced her. She summoned up some level of commitment and said, "That's right... If you harm my daughter or husband, I will cut you down with everything I have."

"Ha-ha... I'll have earned it."

"My name...is Sayaka Sonohara."

The name jolted him.

Sonohara.

The name of the antiques dealer he was just about to go beat up.

"Well, well... I guess it's fate. You just saved your hubby."

"Huh?"

"Never mind. Talking to myself." He smirked. Then he turned his back on the slasher and walked away from the scene. "My name's Akabayashi. Let me know if you ever get tired of that husband of yours."

"Believe me, I'm a worthy enough man to take care of both you *and* your daughter."

♂♀

Present day, Ikebukuro, taxi

"*Yo, Akabayashi,*" said a familiar voice over the phone.

"Is that you, Aozaki? You really do love calling me when I'm in a taxi, don't you?"

"*I don't give a damn about your schedule or where you are.*"

"So what's the call about, then? If it's about the young miss, things have calmed down a bit."

"*Nah. I just called to say my farewell,*" said the low-pitched, jovial voice through the phone.

"Why's that? You gonna kill me once and for all? Or are you staging a mutiny and leaving the Awakusu-kai?"

"*Don't be a moron. You know there's nothing to be gained in that.*"

"Of course not. If there's one thing that's real about you, it's your devotion to Chairman Awakusu."

"*Just shut up and listen,*" Aozaki snapped in irritation. "*You've been living too free these days.*"

*   *   *

"Those ghosts from five years ago have come back to destroy you."

♂♀

May 5, night, ruined building

Quite a ways away from the center of the city stood an unfinished building, its construction halted for some reason or another.

The first two floors were finished like any other building, but everything above that was stuck in skeletal form, the concrete bars standing open in the air and looming eerily over the night.

Men quietly surrounded the building.

"That him?"

"Yep, it's him."

The men in hoodies had bandannas wrapped around their faces. What little skin could be seen of their arms and necks featured fake tattoo stickers with similar patterns. They carried metal pipes, knives, two-by-fours studded with nails, and other crude weapons. These weren't youngsters about to enjoy a spooky rite of passage at a haunted abandoned building—they were outfitted to bust those ghosts themselves.

"I can't believe we're gettin' paid two hundred thousand just to wax that old man."

"Even better, they said they're also gonna give us the lion's share of the shipment when we re-up."

"I heard they were gonna raise our commission on deals."

The information each of them possessed was varied and wild-eyed, but the tattoo-stickered men all shared one particular fact: Their job was to go into the abandoned building and kill the man named Akabayashi.

Hardly any of them knew that he was a lieutenant of the Awakusu-kai. For the most part, they were unaware of the Awakusu-kai at all. But they were drug dealers drawn to a reward for killing a man, so it was possible that even if they *did* know what the Awakusu-kai was, they would still leap at the offer.

In essence, they were the lowest, most disposable pawns in the drug operation. But here they were, right at the destination of their target.

"Man, the Dollars are so useful," one of them said, staring at his phone. Earlier this evening, he posted to the Dollars' message board a picture of Akabayashi attached, saying, "I'm looking for this man. I owe him my life, but I don't know where to find him! Let me know if you see him, so I can thank him!"

And in the very same evening, they found out that he used this abandoned building as a hideout.

"Just when I figured we'd never find his lair, it turns out he's doin' a homeless gig."

"I dunno, man, I heard he's crazy tough."

"Nah, no worries," said another of the gang. He held up a cylindrical object: a Molotov cocktail. "I brought a couple of these, so we can just burn the building down."

He seemed gung ho on the idea, and the others laughed and agreed that it was a good plan. Some of them grabbed the bottles with eyes glazed over; they'd clearly been dipping into their product.

"So once he runs outta the building, we just nab him, take him out into the hills, and...end of story."

"Exactly."

"Let's burn it down."

They all laughed, including the ones who still looked sober. In that sense, from the moment they put on fake tattoos, they were already losing their grip on reality.

♂♀

The same moment, inside

"...I can't believe you'd show yourself like this, Akabayashi," said a stone-faced man, sitting on a toppled oil drum inside the abandoned building. There were nearly a dozen men with him, all clearly members of the underworld.

Standing across from them, dressed as usual with walking stick in hand, was Akabayashi. He maintained his breezy, aloof manner in the face of their open loathing and said, "Well, it's a summons from the gentlemen who taught me so much, back in the day. I can't just blow that off."

"You talk different than you used to. Was that all just an act to fool us back then? Or are you playing coy like this now so you can devour the Awakusu from the inside like you did to us?"

"Actually, you may be surprised to learn that people change and grow. I always assumed that I would be the same person forever after I hit twenty…but the thing is, shocking experiences have a way of changing you," he announced, rapping the floor with his stick. "Such as being attacked by a slasher on the street or falling in love with a woman at first sight for the first time in your life."

"Cut the bull—"

"On the other hand, you said you wanted to talk one-on-one, but it looks like you've got quite a gathering of familiar faces here. Unless I'm mistaken or hallucinating?" Akabayashi said, cracking his neck as he surveyed the group.

The other man's expression softened a bit. "That's right, I'm the only one talking. No guarantees about anything else, though."

"Ah, I see. I didn't see any cars around the building, though. Did you all walk here?"

"…?"

The confident smile never left Akabayashi's face, even in his present danger. The other man cautiously replied, "No…we thought you might get spooked and run. So we parked them a ways off. But I didn't really think you'd show up. If necessary, we were going to rustle up someone you knew and kidnap them as a hostage."

"Which is exactly what I showed up to prevent. But it helps that you don't have cars," Akabayashi said, scratching his cheek. His grin deepened.

"…?"

"Well, if you had lots of cars around, you might get spooked and run, after all."

"What the…hell are you talking about?"

"My line of thought was the same as yours. Yeah, we can talk one-on-one, but I'm not so much of a hero that I'd bother to fight you all on my own."

"?!"

Suspicion flitted across their faces.

Did the Awakusu betray us?

They tensed up, preparing for some sudden sign, but they still needed to find out what Akabayashi was really doing.

"So…you really don't realize that the Awakusu left you out to dry, do you, Akabayashi?"

"What's that? You already cleared this up with the boss?" he replied.

Now the other man was truly confused. "The Awakusu-kai will not interfere with you and me in any way. You might have thought you called for backup, but no one's going to—"

Ktok.

Right in the middle of the man's menacing speech, Akabayashi cut him off by rapping the bottom of the stick on the floor.

"Ha-ha-ha. When did I say anything about the Awakusu-kai?"

"?!"

"It never occurred to you that I might have connections beyond just the Awakusu?"

"No way…!"

Belatedly, the men reassessed the fact that they had called Akabayashi here to make him pay the price for killing their old boss. A nasty sweat broke out on their backs.

Did he bring in yet another yakuza gang…?

"…You're bluffing."

"Think so? Go ahead and look out the window," Akabayashi taunted.

The man glanced over at one of his companions, signaling that he should look outside. The bald man sucked in his breath and headed for the window. He approached the empty window frame carefully, keeping his weight low as he watched for snipers.

Suddenly, the room was full of the sound of breaking glass.

But the building was incomplete, and there were no panes in the windows. The source of the sound was soon quite apparent.

The man with the shaved head instantly began to scream, his body enveloped in flames.

"Aaauuughh! Gaaaaahhhh!"

Some kind of liquid was spreading on the ground, and a second later, it, too, was ablaze.

They realized it was a Molotov cocktail immediately, but before their bodies could react to that knowledge, more flaming bottles entered through the window, shattering in rhythm.

"Outside! There are people outside!" screamed the bald man, who had succeeded in putting out the flames on his face by rolling on the ground. Just before the first bottle had hit him, he'd seen a crowd of figures surrounding the building.

Some of the men inside rushed farther to the back of the room, while others headed for the window on the opposite side. One of them put his back to the wall, peering through the window from the side—and pulled out a gun.

Without hesitation, he started firing into the crowd outside.

♂♀

When the very first *pop* went off, the drug dealers assumed that something inside the building must have exploded. They only realized their mistake when one of them trembled and crumpled to the ground.

"H-hey, what just…?"

"Oh, G-God, my…my leg…"

There was a round hole in the thigh of his jeans, with a red stain spreading outward from it. They only realized it was a bullet wound when the second and third shots rang out.

"Oh, shit! It's a gun! Holy shit, the guy's packin'!"

"Kill him!"

Foolish as it was, they were still under the mistaken assumption that they were dealing with a single man. If they were at least professionals used to undertaking an attack of this sort, they might have scouted out the place and made sure to confirm a number inside. But not only were they rank amateurs, they also weren't even all sober. The gang was in no state to carry out their mission.

Those few who were in a proper state of mind wisely fled the scene, but most of the agitated men decided instead to charge into the building in search of vengeance.

A small war had just erupted, here in this building far from the center of the city…

And neither side understood who it was they were fighting.

♂♀

Inside the chaotic, flaming building, the man who had faced off with Akabayashi bellowed, "Akabayashi, you son of a bitch! You set us up!"

The ex-con looked around, but there was no sight of his foe anywhere. As a matter of fact, Akabayashi had slipped out at the moment the bald man first caught flame and drew the attention of all his fellows.

"I *knew* you killed the boss, Akabayashiii!"

From where he was standing, the man in question murmured, "It wasn't me."

He was leaving the building via the back door, as nonchalantly as if nothing was happening. "I just *let it happen.*"

On the ground at his feet were two men with fake tattoos, who were supposed to be guarding the door. Once he had put a little distance between himself and the building, he saw several police cars drive past.

"Oooh, there they go. Perfect timing—glad I reported it ahead of time," he said, hiding out of sight as the cars passed. He started down a back alley to get farther from the scene. Inside one of the cars, an officer had the receiver in his hand, probably to report a confirmation of the burning building and gunshots.

Akabayashi headed away, pulling out his phone to check the Dollars' home page and delete his own post reading, *"Oh, I know him. He's staying at an abandoned building here on the map in this link."*

The post had a picture of the building, too. He deleted it all, shut off his burner phone, and returned it to his pocket.

Then he looked up at the night sky, wearing his usual smirk, and muttered to himself.

"Yeah, the Dollars are useful. But truth is they're also pretty scary."

♂♀

May 6, morning, Awakusu-kai headquarters

"Skirmish breaks out between criminal organization and youth gang! Sixteen injured! Mass arrests in the middle of the night!"

The tabloid front page blared the latest lurid news, behind which an elderly man murmured, "Oh, look at this, Aozaki. Ruri Hijiribe's going to put out a photo album."

He was looking at the celebrity news page, totally unrelated to the front-page article, and cackled, "There'll be a three-thousand-unit limited edition, too. That'll fetch a good price. Couldn't ya just buy 'em all up and sell 'em on that *hee-bay* thing?!"

"I don't know… I'm not the right guy to ask about that. Check with Shiki or Kazamoto…"

"Ahh. Well, at any rate, tell one of the kids to go and buy three for me."

"Please, boss, think of your age. You gotta set an example for the young guys," Aozaki pleaded. He glanced at the front page of the newspaper held open across from him. "So, boss…did you know this would happen?"

He was referring to the outcome of the two incidents involving Akabayashi, of course. All those men fresh out of jail who had gone after him were promptly arrested again. The kids with the fake tats were all rounded up, too, which would certainly set off quite a lot of police and media investigation into the student-run gang.

While neither group was a real enemy to the Awakusu-kai, the incident certainly cleared two potential annoyances out of their hair and had the added bonus of drawing police attention away from them for a time.

Without taking his eyes off the paper, Dougen Awakusu answered, "I had a hunch. A bit of this, a bit of that. I knew that Akabayashi could handle his own matters—and it seems that someone else was watching out for him, too."

"…Whatever do you mean?"

"I suspect someone tipped him off that he was being targeted. He couldn't have arranged such an elaborate trap in advance without knowing about it," Dougen commented, his eye peering over the top of the paper at Aozaki.

"I don't know who would have done such a thing, sir...but I suspect that since we weren't going to take *action*, that person figured words didn't count."

"Hah! Never took you for the type to tell jokes. So you wanted to settle your score with Akabayashi yourself, huh?"

"Now you're the one joking, boss," Aozaki replied, shaking his head with a grin. "Maybe in the old days, but now that he's gone soft, there's no point to killing him."

"You know, soft can be a good thing, too. Lots of stuff bounces off you when you're soft..."

The phone on the desk rang. Dougen fumbled the receiver loose, cleared his throat, and put it to his ear. From Aozaki's position, what sounded like a scream of anguish squeaked through the speaker. Perhaps the brand-new gang that got itself arrested last night was now calling for help.

Dougen maintained the same cold, steady tone of voice he always did when on the phone. "Why, I don't know what you mean. We said we wouldn't take action against you, and that was that. If you tried to attack Akabayashi and wound up in a trap, that's none of my concern."

They were no fools. They were men of the night, responsible for building the darkness of Ikebukuro.

Dougen ended the call and returned to his newspaper—with a sadistic smile on his lips this time.

"You see, I can't betray my trading partners...but I can abandon them."

♂♀

Five years ago

The man changed after his meeting with the slasher.

He told people that he'd been attacked by the slasher but made up the details: "It was a huge old man, over six feet tall, with white hair."

He was actually just quoting a manga he'd read recently, but no one recognized it, so the others within the group merely laughed and said, "Turns out he's human after all."

Because of his injury, he got a temporary reprieve on the Sonohara-dou job. He'd started the job, and he would finish it, he said. So he spent his time investigating the business, trying to find a way to save them—to save that beautiful, bewitching slasher…

One day, he learned that the slasher had struck at Sonohara-dou, killing the two parents.

The husband's head was lopped clean off, while the wife's stomach was slit in a manner resembling seppuku.

The daughter was still alive but in a state of terrible shock, unable to speak.

When he heard about it, he couldn't believe it at first.

A terrible sense of loss infused his entire being. It was far worse than the feeling of losing his eye—it felt like his entire life was being ripped away.

But through his grief, he knew.

He knew that the wife, Sayaka Sonohara, had committed suicide.

She *was* the slasher, after all. Whatever happened, she ended up cutting off the head of the husband she loved, then turned the blade on her own belly.

But why had she done it?

Weren't her husband and daughter equally precious to her?

It wasn't the entire family, just her husband, who she killed before committing suicide, leaving only the daughter alive. Whatever could have happened to her body?

He was temporarily broken out of this train of unanswered questions by the sound of his boss's voice.

"Hey, Akabayashi. No need to worry about Sonohara-dou anymore."

"…Sir?"

Akabayashi was often tapped to serve as the yakuza boss's bodyguard, in recognition of his skill. Today, the boss was heading to his favorite lady companion's house alone, taking only the one guard.

"The people who own Sonohara-dou are both dead, as you know. And now we get the land without having to deal with them. Long live the slasher!"

"…"

"Whoops. I shouldn't have mentioned that—forgot you lost your eye to him," the boss said, a distasteful sneer on his face. "But the place would've been done for in either case."

"…?"

"I gave the owner a little taste of medicine, you see."

"…?!"

It was obvious what he meant by "medicine."

Akabayashi had always hated drugs. As a man to whom strength and violence were everything, the idea of making your own bones more brittle was unfathomable to him. He didn't have a crusade to stop the gang from doing its drug business; he just didn't bother to think about it.

The boss cackled with delight and explained, "We already had a contract that gave us the right to seize his land as collateral, but I figured we could squeeze more out of him… So I made him an offer. Take out life insurance on your family and let's make some money, I said."

"…!"

"From what I hear, he was always the violent type at home. But once he got hooked on the dope, it got way worse. That stuff must've really fucked with his head," his boss bragged—he'd probably had a few drinks. "They didn't put this in the papers, but from what I heard, the kid had marks around her neck. The police thought it was the slasher who did it, but I'm betting that at some point, the old man tried to strangle his own daughter! All to raise the money to support his drug habit!"

"…"

"See? Crazy, right? You're not gonna get the insurance if you kill the brat yourself! But maybe he actually thought he might get away with it? In either case, it's laughable."

The yakuza boss might as well have been intoxicated on his own speech. He wasn't paying any attention to his surroundings.

"The thing is, that kid looked like she'd grow up to be a pretty fine-lookin' woman herself! I figured I could whip up a convincing little IOU form and collect on the girl—she could make us a fortune! Maybe I could even get first dibs? Then again, she's only what, twelve? Can't have much experience yet, gah-ha-ha!"

There were a number of things the boss wasn't paying attention to—that he *failed* to pay attention to.

One: the increasingly icy manner of the bodyguard charged with attending to his safety.

Two: the fact that they were in a totally empty back alley.

And three: that a man with a knife was approaching with murder in his eyes.

"Hmm...?"

At last, the boss noticed the third of these details. The man with the knife stared at the gleeful yakuza, seething with hatred.

"You bastard..."

"Who the hell are you? Who're you with?!" the boss demanded.

But the tear-streaked young man with the knife responded, "You'll pay...for what you did...to my sister..."

"Huh...? Oh, I get it. You must be that one girl's brother. Yeah, now I remember seeing you in that family photo she carried around."

"You got her hooked...on your damn drugs! It's all because of you! Now they say...she might never wake up and walk around again!"

Apparently, the interloper had a score to settle with the boss over the gang's drug-dealing operation.

"Hah! If anything, you should be *thanking* me for letting her last memories be blissful, then! C'mon, Akabayashi, do your job. Grab this ungrateful little shithead and squeeze the life outta...ah...ah... ah..."

He spun around to give Akabayashi his orders but froze in place.

As the saying goes, one can look down on another person like an ant—but in Akabayashi's case, the gaze he was giving the shorter man was full of such disgust and anger that he might as well have been trying to squash that ant through visual pressure alone.

The gaze was so strong that the boss felt as though his shoulders were being held down. All that unstoppable pressure was emanating from the prosthetic right eye.

"Wh-what the hell…are you staring at me…like that…for…?"

He could barely even form the words to accost his subordinate. The pressure flowing from Akabayashi was so all-consuming that the boss completely forgot that he was in a dire situation that allowed for no distractions.

Several minutes later, the yakuza boss was lying facedown in the street, twitching. Red liquid pooled beneath his upper half.

A short ways away, the young man trembled, his knife dripping with blood.

"…"

Akabayashi took a step closer, causing the boy to turn the knife toward him. But either he instinctively realized he didn't stand a chance against a much larger man, or he was satisfied at completing his revenge; in any case, the young man sat down on the spot.

"Kill me… Just kill me already! I can't… There's nothing I—"

Akabayashi slapped him. "If you die, who's going to take care of your sister? Huh?"

"…! …? H…huh?"

The boy turned his trembling face to look up at Akabayashi. He clearly didn't understand what the man was saying.

"Just…go. Hide the knife and get out of here. If you're lucky, they'll chalk this one up to the slasher."

"…?! Ah…aaah… Th-tha…thank you!" he stammered, getting to his feet and hiding the knife under his shirt.

No doubt the young man had no idea why his life was being spared, but hearing the word *sister* had brought some measure of control back to his mind and spurred him away from the scene.

"'Thank you'?" Akabayashi murmured, looking down at the corpse of his boss. "Don't thank me, kid… You should hate me."

"I just turned you into a murderer…"

♂♀

Present day, near a Yamanote Line station, shopping district backstreet

"Ooh, Ruri's got a photo album coming out? Better get my preorder in."

Akabayashi strode down the street, reading the same tabloid as Dougen Awakusu had.

Suddenly, his eye stopped on a particular word in the article. "Oh, right, she changed agencies. And they haven't found Yodogiri yet? Guess Shiki's got his hands full."

The word in question was the name of Ruri Hijiribe's new talent agency. "*Jack-o'-Lantern*, huh?"

It was a very peculiar and memorable name, but Akabayashi snorted and thought, *Hell, it's me.*

While it wasn't widely known in Japan, a jack-o'-lantern was a pumpkin-faced spirit often associated with Halloween. It started off as an Irish legend: a human turned away from heaven for his wicked deeds but also shunned from hell for cheating the devil and therefore doomed to wander the earth as a ghost forever, carrying a lantern carved from a pumpkin.

In the world of the yakuza, the most forbidden act was to kill one's parent—the boss.

Akabayashi didn't do the deed himself, but there was no denying that he abandoned his boss to a certain death. Naturally, he wasn't going to wind up in heaven, either.

He was something like a ghost, unable to exist fully in the light or the darkness, wandering aimlessly.

Maybe calling myself a jack-o'-lantern is a stretch. That's cooler than I deserve.

Akabayashi chuckled as he walked along the street, paced from behind by a smaller figure.

This sneaking follower carried the sharp glint of a knife in its hands.

However...

"Yah!"

"!"

Akabayashi knew he was being trailed. He spun around, grabbed his assailant's hand, and snatched the knife right out of it.

It turned out to be a boy, maybe fifteen years old.

"Come on, kids should be kids, not playing with toys like this. Go back home and play some video games. You can't hurt anyone doing that."

"*Eep!* Aa...aaah!"

The boy raced away. Akabayashi watched him go and tucked the knife into his pocket. "Hmm... Does a small knife count as recyclable? Or is it classified as metal garbage?"

He wondered about the boy. There had been a tattoo sticker on his neck, which meant he was one of the remaining members of that gang. Or perhaps he was hoping to get in, and they ordered him to stab Akabayashi as a means of initiation.

I'll be damned. If it weren't for the fake tat, I really would have no idea.

He considered the Dollars and the way Anri reacted yesterday and couldn't help but feel that something in the atmosphere of the city was eerily lukewarm.

It's like the kids these days really don't know how to tell the difference between day and night. Not that a pumpkin head like me has any room to call them out.

He murmured, "Still, I'm allowed to pray."

If possible, I'd like to at least keep the boundary between day and night clear—so that Anri and Miss Akane can avoid being collateral damage.

He thought about the daughter of the first woman he ever loved. The way she was growing up to resemble her mother reminded him of the slasher.

Maybe...

Just maybe, if he continued wandering the boundary line between hell and heaven like a jack-o'-lantern, he might one day run into that slasher again.

That's stupid. I must be reading too much manga.

He smirked at himself again, rapped his walking stick, and continued on his way.

"But if the girls say they prefer the night...well, it ain't my place to stop them."

*   *   *

And so, the man began to walk as the sun set,
Following the boundary line between the light side of town and the dark.

With the scar of his first-sight love burned permanently into one eye,
The man once more vanished into the depths of the city, smiling easily.

Ordinary C

Collection

Rhapsody

At first, the rumors were absolutely true.

"Hey, did you hear?"

"You mean Shizuo Heiwajima?"   "It's Shizuo."   "Him."

"Walking around with a girl."   "Shizuo Heiwajima."

"Maybe nine years old."

"Heard he fought with yakuza."

"Climbed a building with his bare hands."

"Heard he kicked a car."   "Got stabbed by a girl."

"But the knife wouldn't sink in; it just clattered onto the ground!"

"They saw him jump from the car carrying a girl."

"He threw a bike one-handed."

"Dude's crazy."

*   *   *

The rumors spread through the Internet, phone calls, and even word of mouth.

Of all the events taking place during May's weeklong holiday, there was a clear, odd pattern.

The topic of one man's extraordinary feats stood out from the others, as though he were rampaging here and there throughout Ikebukuro without rest.

By default, he was a notable sight in Ikebukuro by virtue of being the "man around town in the bartender's outfit." Normally, that could also apply to street barkers and the like, but because he also featured blond hair, sunglasses, and a dreadlocked partner, he was always immediately identified as a man to stay away from.

However, the more someone got to know him, the more their approach and assessment of his character changed.

"Shouldn't be approached" could turn into "Do not approach at any cost," "Nicer than I thought," "Run at first sight," "Get down and beg," "Give up," or any number of other options—varied but always extreme.

In the same way someone might describe a monster that no one else had ever seen, these extreme opinions led to equally extreme rumors, placing severe stress upon the *actual facts* of the matter.

"Hey, did you hear?"

"You know that Shizuo Heiwajima guy?"   "That monster."

"I heard he died."

"Got smashed by a car."   "Trying to protect a girl."

"Hit by a dump truck."   "Shizuo."   "It was him."

"Ran into a motorcycle."   "The yakuza pushed him off a rooftop."

"He died from getting stabbed by a woman."   "No shit."

"He has a kid."

*　　*　　*

"Isn't that crazy?"

All of it was nonsense.

And in terms of extremes, the one phrase—"Shizuo died"—was so shocking to most that it spread with incredible speed.

As that message outpaced the rest, the rumors underwent corrections.

Would Shizuo Heiwajima die from being hit by a car?

Clearly not, according to the people who knew Shizuo best or followed rumors about him the most.

Shizuo Heiwajima would not die from something like that, they knew, which necessitated a correction to the rumor.

Through the logic, biases, and desires of a great many people, the rumors were buffeted and sanded down to one unified form.

A rumor that has spread too far can become an urban legend.

And when an urban legend gains the clarity of form, it spreads even further and deeper.

For example, among young delinquents at a club.

"…Hey, you hear?"

"'Bout what?"

"Shizuo Heiwajima."

"…What about that monster?"

"He…got hit by a truck, and he's really hurt."

"…For real?"

"Yeah. *He was on the run from the yakuza, jumped off a building, and then…wham.*"

"So…he's all torn up right now, huh?"

For example, among drug dealers hoping to eliminate Shizuo and gain notoriety for themselves.

"But I heard he's still up and walking around like normal."

"I don't care how hurt he is—I ain't gonna pick a fight with him while he's still got all his limbs."

"I ain't afraid, I'm just sayin', you gotta be sure you can kill him…"

"In that case, I got something else for ya."

"What's that?"

"He got himself a girl."

"No way?!"

"I hear he's been walking around the city with a girl."

For example, among the remnants of a street gang Shizuo once crushed.

"...If you ask me, Shizuo being weakened is a once-in-a-lifetime opportunity..."

"You don't know, he might have just been showing that girl around town..."

"No, get this! Turns out that chick is damaged goods."

"Huh?"

"I'm serious—Shizuo's got a kid! A kid old enough to be in school!"

"Are you crazy?!"

"I mean, how old is that guy?!"

"I bet he went out with her back in high school, when he was the biggest player. Then she shows up after a few years and goes, 'The kid is yours!'"

All of it was nonsense, but in the end, they'd all believe the rumors.

And that was because those rumors stimulated a *desire* deep within their hearts. It was less that they firmly believed the stories than that they clung to them, in their wish for them to be true.

Because the ultimate desire of all those who believed the rumors was...

"...Do you think...right now..."

"...we might have a shot at Shizuo Heiwajima?"

The rumors had only been around for a single day.

But they succeeded at spurring certain people into action.

Action that could only lead to their downfall, according to those who knew the truth.

♂♀

May 5, day, Ikebukuro, old apartment

Loud rapping upon the front door disturbed the quiet of the apartment, a shabby place at least thirty years old.

"Mr. Sugawa? I know you're there, Sandayuu Sugawa," came a young man's voice between the rhythmic pounding of the fist. After a brief pause, the door opened up, revealing a very sickly face.

"Good afternoon. I think you know why I'm here," said the man with dreadlocks, grimacing, running through his protocol. Behind him, a man in a bartender's uniform yawned. He had blond hair and sunglasses, making him look just like a bodyguard.

As the terrified young man stared out at them, the one who knocked said, "Well, let's get that money, shall we?"

Tom Tanaka was a debt collector.

But it wasn't for shady black market lenders. He belonged to a company that had contracts with a wide variety of slightly more reputable businesses: brothels, sex hotlines, singles websites, rental video shops.

Such businesses sometimes needed to collect late fees or unpaid bills from their customers, and so Tom's company was called on to perform this step—all within legal boundaries.

Of course, some types of debt collection could only be performed through a lawyer, and as far as the video rentals went, they didn't know if the shops actually had the permits required to do that business. So Tom operated in a kind of gray zone that was actually not that ambiguous in the least, much like the unsavory loopholes exploited by pachinko parlors to function as gambling dens.

If it was the type of job where they took money from seniors without families, Tom and the bartender-looking man with him, Shizuo Heiwajima, would have quit ages ago. But there was no common sympathy for those who failed to pay for their sex hotlines and porn tape rentals.

Perhaps if someone tried the hackneyed, old "I'm trying to find my long-lost sister" excuse for calling the hotlines, they would at least do their due diligence in trying to determine the truth, but Tom had never run across someone attempting to use that line.

They didn't try to pretend that it was a social good they were performing, but otherwise, it was like pretty much any other job.

On the other hand, some of those late on their payments never intended to pay up, and out of that group, there was always a percentage engaging in illegal activities, so the job was not without its risks. Therefore, Tom regularly performed his duties with his bodyguard-slash-assistant, Shizuo Heiwajima.

"Listen, if you want, we can take this to court and have the whole matter cleared up. But neither of us have time for that, do we? We're not ripping you off; we didn't charge more than was explained to you. And come on, man—the money's one thing, but at *least* return the tape, yeah? It's two hundred yen per day, so how many tapes did you borrow to rack up one hundred fifty thousand in debt?!"

"W-w-wait, wait! I never said I wouldn't pay up! I have the tapes I copied up in an online auction now! Once I get the money for that, I can pay you back!"

"Are you dubbing our—? All right, cut the shit and stop messing with the business model. Listen, I'll ignore that for today, but I need one or the other: money or tapes."

Tom got tired of arguing and tried to wrap up the process, realizing that he was dealing with a more miserable scumbag than he figured. He started to step inside, but the man pushed him back and wheedled, "W-w-wait, please! All right! I'll pay, I'll pay!"

"That's better. And if you're short, you can take out a high-interest loan to make up the difference."

Wow, he sure broke quickly, Tom thought. But then the creep smirked over Tom's shoulder toward the man standing out in the apartment hallway.

"Hey, what about you? Why don't *you* pay the late fee for me, Shizuo Heiwajima?"

"Wait, don't—" Tom panicked.

"*What?*" Shizuo asked icily, turning his head with an eyebrow raised.

Oh, shit. This can't be good, Tom thought, sensing that Shizuo could explode in mere seconds. He stepped away from the door, sidling up to his partner and asking, "Let me just ask…do you know this guy?"

"Nope…never seen him before in my life," Shizuo replied brusquely.

The man inside smirked. "You're a famous guy—everyone knows you. I could tell immediately from the outfit."

"Oh yeah…?" Shizuo said, clearly getting angrier. Tom inched farther away from the two.

The oblivious debtor was paving his own path to hell. "You're Yuuhei Hanejima's brother, isn't that right?"

"…!"

Don't—! Tom nearly screamed. *…Wait a second, why have I never heard that?*

"Oh yeah…? And what if I am his brother?"

"He's superrich, isn't he? I bet you get a little tiny cut of that fortune. You must have a little chump change lying around."

Damn, if I knew this guy was suicidal, I would've had Shizuo wait farther away!

Tom retreated down the apartment steps until he had evacuated to the ground level—right around the time the man delivered his clinching remark.

"So if you don't want all the tabloids to find out that he's got a thug of a brother like you, you'd better pay my—"

The only thing it clinched was his own downfall, however.

There was the hollow sound of some piece of a whole being removed, right at the same time that the man stopped talking. Shizuo had grabbed the man's face with one hand and instantly separated his jaw.

"…What was that about money?"

He let go, and the indebted man's jaw hung loose. The mouth was gaping wide enough to fit a fist inside. His jaw quivered in the air like a cat's cradle; he reached up to touch it but seemed not to understand yet what had happened.

"Ah, agagagah, agah?"

"I've heard enough from you. Now shut your filthy mouth."

"Ah, agaaa! Agagagagah!" the man stammered, unable to actually close his mouth. Shizuo took a step forward.

"…I said…*shut it!*"

* * *

Tom heard him from outside the apartment building. The next moment, there was a violent crash. He looked up to see a second-floor window smash.

The reason why soon became apparent.

The body of the man who owed them money flew through the shattering glass, smashed into a tree planted on the apartment lot, and then fell next to Tom, breaking a few branches along the way.

His clothes happened to catch on the branches, so he wound up hanging at eye level with Tom, who surveyed the debtor with pity.

"Hey, you lucked out."

"H-h-hewp… I—I'll tell the cops…I—I—I'll sue…"

His jaw was miraculously fitted back into place, so perhaps Shizuo had given him an uppercut. Tom looked at the ghastly man with the trembling voice and calmly asked, "And what story are you going to give to the cops?"

"…Eh?"

"Perhaps you'll tell them, 'I got in trouble for borrowing pornos and making illegal copies to sell online, so I tried to blackmail the collector and got beat up'? I'd pay to see that trial. We could invite your dad and mom to come see you plead your case."

"…!"

"But if you're smart enough to decide that you don't want to be famous for the wrong reasons, we'll be nice enough to pay for your broken window," Tom said, brushing his dreads off his ears and shrugging.

"It's only getting tacked on to your late fees, though."

♂♀

Ten minutes later, Ikebukuro

"Dammit, just because you're not killing them doesn't make this right."

"…Sorry, Tom."

They were on their way back to Ikebukuro Station from the collection spot, and Tom had been lecturing Shizuo about what went wrong.

"You bend a five-hundred-yen coin in front of their eyes to intimidate them so that you don't *have* to resort to violence! In fact, I bet you could tear one of those coins in two with your fingers, right?"

"Yeah...but I'm pretty sure I heard that it's against the law to bend or stretch coins like that."

"What...? Oh, true. Good point. Well, we can think of another method," Tom admitted, bringing the conversation to an awkward, temporary truce. They walked through the crowd, thinking hard.

"Man, that guy really was an idiot, wasn't he? He knew who you were, and he went ahead and threatened you... In fact, it was kinda like he didn't know anything about you *except* that you're Kasuka's brother."

"...I suppose you're right."

"The funny thing is, any street punk worth his salt would give up just by looking at you...but lately, you get the occasional normal person who has no idea about what you're like and feels foolhardy..."

"...Sorry," Shizuo muttered.

Tom turned to him in surprise. "Why are you apologizing?"

"Uh...I just figured, if I was keeping control of myself better..."

"Yeah, but that has nothing to do with the fact that there are total idiots like that guy. I know I gave you that lecture, but honestly, you did pretty good back there. In fact, it kind of makes me sorry for getting you involved in this dangerous line of work," Tom said, facing forward again.

Shizuo watched his boss from behind and said, "Thank you," but he didn't seem to be quite convinced himself.

Tom sighed and then checked his watch. "It's a bit early, but I suppose we could get something to eat."

"Let's hit up Russia Sushi and have ourselves a feast."

Russia Sushi

She was in a very bad mood.

There was sadness, anger, and frustration mixed together and brought to a boil, then pushed down where it couldn't get out—until nothing showed on her face but the faintest trace of sullenness.

But thanks to her already attractive features, the look could also be interpreted as mournful.

The white man behind the sushi counter stared back at that grimace and said, "Hey, Vorona. This is a service business. Stop sulking, or you'll drive our customers off."

"...Negative. My face is not crafted in melancholy. It is as normal," said the woman named Vorona, albeit in rather odd Japanese.

A large black man cleaning tables smiled amiably and said, "Oh, that no good, Vorona. That face bad. Customer is God. God must be forgiving. If patient Buddha only forgives three times, then God must forgive hundred times. One hundred trips to pray to Ebisu, god of luck and good business. So smile wide like Ebisu."

"Meaning unclear. Semyon's Japanese is a bizarre fantasy."

The man behind the counter mumbled, "Look who's talking," but Vorona ignored him and looked away, stone-faced.

"Besides...I have just abandoned my partner. Impossible to reach that circumstance."

Vorona was a freelance *jack-of-all-trades* contractor.

Since coming to Japan, she'd worked for a variety of people and committed every sort of crime. Assassination, weapons smuggling, kidnapping—if the police ever caught her, she'd spend the rest of her life behind bars or be extradited back to Russia.

With her partner, Slon, she'd been working primarily in Ikebukuro, but after drawing the ire of a local yakuza group, the Awakusu-kai, Slon's legs got shot up. They took him away, and Vorona determined that it was best not to hold out hope that he was alive.

As for her...

...

Rather suddenly, she realized that her unhappiness was not out of grief for Slon.

The owner of the shop sharpened his knife and said, "But you must have known that this would happen. From what I hear, you lost three other companions before making it to Japan. If you didn't bother getting vengeance for them, why get all worked up about revenge for this particular partner?"

"...If the time exists to perish, I am first. That was my assurance. In my home country, one foolish enemy was sloppy for the reason that I am a woman. As a result, Slon and I live," she mumbled, mostly to herself. Her head dipped. "This time is further worse. In the instant we should have died together, I was allowed to live through Father's benevolence... It is humiliation."

In fact, she was under a crippling amount of stress—but not because she'd lost her partner.

If she were the type to treasure the lives of others, she wouldn't have gotten involved in this business in the first place.

It was simply that she wasn't able to forgive herself.

I want to destroy everything. Including myself.

She'd been overcome by the urge right after she woke up, mere hours ago. That initial impulse would have been carried out violently if it weren't for the two Russia Sushi employees who were there to hold her down.

"Calm down," Denis had told her in Russian. "Go ahead and get your revenge on the Awakusu-kai if you must, but don't wreck up our place."

Strangely, that brief statement was all it took for her to wrestle her impulse under control.

"Am I...weak?" she asked.

Denis said, "You're not stronger than Drakon," and Simon told her, "We're not the ones to decide that." Pondering the meaning of that helped to restore her sense of rationality.

She asked if it was possible to rescue Slon, knowing it wasn't—and so the replies she got were unsatisfying. She understood why it was happening.

"Not having anything to do will fill your mind with pointless thoughts," Denis and Simon said and told her to help out around the restaurant.

Vorona didn't consider this to be a cold suggestion. When she worked for Colonel Lingerin, it was quite common for people to die during routine jobs, so even on the rare occasions one had time to mourn the dead, it was always while on the move.

She decided that letting her emotions rule her was pointless and unproductive and decided to follow their suggestion. However...

Me, a waitress? It's ridiculous.

She surveyed the restaurant, wearing a feminine uniform. The interior should have been strongly reminiscent of home, but given that it was all in service of being a sushi place, there was no denying the alien feeling.

It was a *wrong* Russia, the kind of Russia you saw in a movie filmed for some far-off country.

President Lingerin would love it, but my father, Drakon, would be annoyed, she thought. Her eyes landed on the two Russians hard at work. *And...why are they doing this in the first place? They must be crazy to set up a restaurant in a place like this.*

All her memories of Denis and Simon were from the distant past. They each had their own history before coming to work for Lingerin's arms company, and then a few years ago, they both abruptly moved here to Japan.

I'm certain that Denis made quite a lot of money working for President Lingerin...but setting up shop in this expensive place would have wiped out almost all his savings.

...Actually, I shouldn't bother trying to figure this out.

After they held her down to calm her this morning, they hadn't bothered to pry into Vorona's business any further. If they weren't going to be nosy, she should at least return the favor.

The problem was, once she drove those thoughts from her head, she had nothing left to do but reflect on the last few days' memories.

What...am I doing?

All she wanted was to determine the strength of humanity. It was a question in her head since childhood that she could never learn from books alone.

And eventually, that question became her reason for living.

But the events of the recent past brought her to a sobering realization: that she might not have the strength needed to learn that truth.

I am weak.

The Black Rider was a true monster and didn't count.

She'd assumed the man in the bartender's suit represented the best possible value for her test. But then, up against the Awakusu-kai man, she'd been utterly helpless.

Then was everything I've done pointless...?

It felt like her pleasure, past, and hope for the future had all been negated, taken away from her. She was filled with anger at her mental vulnerability for feeling this way and her physical weakness at being unable to save one man.

These thoughts swirled through her head as she stood in place.

Denis told her to "watch them work and steal their ideas," but she didn't know where to start with that. For one thing, she had zero service industry experience. She had read about some of its secrets in books, but she had never seen a business that combined Russia with sushi, in real life or in any text.

On the other hand...

She'd been merely standing in place, observing everything that happened from the moment the restaurant opened—and realized that the guests seemed to be extraordinarily preoccupied with *her*.

Is it so strange for them to see a foreigner? But that applies to Denis and Simon, too.

It never even occurred to her that it had something to do with her looks and feminine gender. Any regular would be surprised at the sudden appearance of an unfamiliar waitress, while a new customer would find it hard *not* to look at the beautiful foreign woman brooding in the corner with her hands on her hips.

Simon turned to a young couple, barely older than children, and said, "Oh, young master Yagiri, you like her? Her name Vorona. You take her to go, A-OK. Then you have girlfriend and mistress, one in each hand. Best to eat with those you love, makes everything taste good. Plus ten orders of sushi."

...I did not hear of taking to go. Is that part of the business plan here? I don't mind doing the same job, assuming a customer respects my talents...but I'm certainly not going to sell my actual body, thought Vorona, who failed to take Simon's comment in jest.

She scowled and said, "Negative. I am under no obligation to sell my own flesh for the profit of the company. I request a boycott. But if your words are meant in the spirit of contract job, I confirm."

"Ohh, this is famous Japanese sexual harassment trial. Sexual harassment bad, no *sekuhara*. If you do *sekuhara*, then you do harakiri. And after cutting stomach, sushi all fall through hole. Our business go up in flames." Simon laughed, but Vorona did not understand what he meant.

The customers who had just been subjected to two very different but equally baffling forms of Japanese reacted with either awkward amusement or total confusion but otherwise kept eating. Vorona sensed their reactions and was coming to the acceptance that she probably wasn't meant for this line of work when Denis spoke to her.

"Hey, Vorona. Collector's out back, so get the white envelope off the office desk and hand it over."

"…"

"If you can't serve customers, you can at least give them the money in the envelope, right?"

"…Affirmative," she admitted, reluctantly passing through the kitchen toward the back.

Next to the back door was a small office. She took the thick envelope off the desk and opened the door.

"Whoa."

There was a familiar man standing there.

"…!"

Instantly, Vorona crouched and swung her leg up to kick at his groin.

"Easy, easy."

He caught the kick soaring upward between his legs with one hand and pushed it back, simultaneously sweeping her planted leg. Vorona quickly found herself sitting flat on her butt, though the man had eased the pressure on her leg so that there was no pain.

"…!"

If only I had a weapon…

It galled Vorona that at this moment, the only idea that came to her mind involved relying on gear. Still, she stared malevolently at the man in the patterned suit.

"Ooh, scary. I figured I'd check in on you when I came to collect the crab money, but I didn't think you'd be the one handing it over. I thought you'd still be bedridden. Suppose I'll have to save the caviar sushi for another time."

"Akabayashi!"

"What, you remember my name? That's so sweet. A guy feels good when a fetching young lady like you is familiar with him," he said, smirking wryly as he reached out to take the envelope from Vorona. Then he turned his back on her, totally unafraid.

"Sorry to disappoint you. I'd give you a little more time, but I've got another young lady to escort at the moment. Maybe some other occasion."

"I request orders! Has Slon already been being killed?"

"Whoa, whoa, slow down. What if someone hears you talking about killing and all that?" he said, looking around hastily before continuing. "Well, I suppose it's up to him whether he gets spared or buried."

"...?"

"At any rate, there's certainly going to be a price paid. Mikiya and Aozaki are pragmatists at heart. They're probably weighing the value of either finishing him off to make things right or keeping him around to use as a pawn."

He tapped his own shoulders with the walking stick, then turned his back on Vorona once again. "Ultimately, it's the chairman who will call the shots. But if your buddy spills the beans on your client, that fella named Yodogiri...well, maybe the scales will tip toward a more amicable outcome."

"..."

Should she rejoice in the possibility of Slon's survival or find some new weapons and raid the Awakusu-kai to rescue him? Vorona couldn't even be sure how she should react to Akabayashi's statement.

Time simply passed. How long had it been?

She glared powerlessly in the direction that Akabayashi had gone, until a cheery voice said, "Oh, here you are. What wrong? Your tummy hurt?"

"...Denied. Woe is fruitless," she replied, getting to her feet as if nothing was wrong.

Simon shrugged and asked, "Did you fight with Akabayashi? Fighting bad, you get hungry. And Akabayashi bring us cheap crabmeat. You make Akabayashi angry, crab get more expensive, us and customers go hungry."

"Is that crab a smuggled good?"

"He said what he send us is national product. He don't say what nation."

"..."

While the conversation was not entirely satisfying, Simon's voice did help her regain herself. She went back inside the building.

I suppose...it's all over.

In that brief period, dark feelings swirled into her mind.

I abandoned plenty of companions on the way here...and I had to be saved by my father and President Lingerin, the men I betrayed and severed all connections to... How do they see me now? With disgust? Or pity?

Perhaps I have no reason to live anymore...

After her consecutive defeats and what Akabayashi just told her, even her motivation to avenge Slon was gone.

No, that was always an excuse. I wasn't nearly as mad about Slon's defeat as I was at my own uselessness. What should I do now...?

She made her way through the kitchen into the restaurant, pondering these heavy topics...

There were now two men sitting at the counter where the young couple had just been.

She recognized one of the men. Not by facial features, but by his distinctive dress.

Even Vorona, who found it quite difficult to distinguish the fine details between Japanese faces, could identify his features at a glance.

He had blond hair and wore sunglasses to go with a bartender's uniform.

"Well, when both you and Kasuka get so famous, you can't prevent guys like that from coming around. I think you ought to get used to this."

"...Okay."

"I know it wasn't your idea to be famous. But I think if you keep that fact in mind, it'll actually make a big difference in your life."

"I guess so..."

Tom and Shizuo had picked up their conversation from earlier as they waited for their sashimi tray.

"By the way, did you thank that doctor from yesterday?" Tom asked.

"...Oh, actually, not yet."

"Well, that won't do. He helped you out in a pinch—I don't care if you guys go way back, he deserves a proper thanks."

"Yeah, you're right. It slipped my mind with all the other stuff going on," Shizuo explained. He took out his phone and called up the black market doctor. "Hey...Shinra? Sorry about yesterday. I wanted to thank you for your help... What? Oh...yeah. I'll call you later, then."

He was going to walk outside to continue the call but never got further than a hovering position above the chair.

"What's up?" Tom asked.

"I guess he's busy. He said to call back tomorrow. In fact...it sounded like he was gonna cry."

"Oh yeah? Well, no rush, I guess. You can do it any...oh?" Tom paused when he saw a woman appear from the kitchen. "Who's the babe? She's staring holes in us."

"...You're right," Shizuo added. "In fact, I don't think she's ever done a shift here before."

Tom glanced at the woman staring at them while her mouth worked silently, then leaned over the counter to ask the chef, "Hey, boss, when'd you pick up that fetching lady? Is she Russian, too?"

"Correct. She's in training—doesn't even know how to carry out a fresh towel. Think of her as a Russian decoration for now," he answered brusquely.

Tom grinned and asked, "How do you say 'You're adorable' in Russian?"

"Вы очаровательны."

"*Vee, ocheravatenen,*" Tom mimicked. Then he turned to the woman. "*Hey, vee ocheravatenen.*"

The white woman looked back at Tom with suspicion and then turned to the chef behind the counter. "What is he saying? It is unclear. Suspicion that words are not Japanese."

The chef smirked and shook his head. "Вы очаровательны."

"...Provide a clear reason that you would engage in such social pleasantries."

"That's just what that fella there said to you."

"In the language of what country?"

Confused and surprised, Tom leaned over to Shizuo and whispered, "Was my pronunciation that bad?"

"I wouldn't know the difference, but I guess a native speaker would."

"Wow, I guess I embarrassed myself," Tom said, trying to hide the redness behind his cup of tea. Just then, the platter of sashimi came across the counter to them.

Tom reached out with his chopsticks, glanced at the woman again, and wondered, "Is she glaring at us or something?"

He almost stopped himself from bringing it up, but he knew that Shizuo wasn't stupid enough to accost a woman for staring at him and so it was safe to proceed.

"Really? Whoa, that's harsh," Shizuo said, his eyes tearing up. He had just eaten a bracing sushi roll stuffed with wasabi. His vision was so blurry that he didn't even bother to look in her direction. "Probably because you did such a bad job hitting on her."

"You think so? Well, yeah...I guess you're right." Tom sighed, grabbing a slice of yellowtail.

The chef leaned forward and said, "By the way...you two said you were short on help recently, didn't cha?"

"Huh? Oh yeah. There's been an uptick in folks trying to welch on their fees, so it's getting hard for me and Shizuo to cover everything on our own." Tom grimaced.

The chef nodded—then glanced over at the woman.

"Feel like taking that decoration off my hands?"

♂♀

Ikebukuro, in front of a dojo

In a mixed zoning area near Zoshigaya Cemetery bustling with apartments, small homes, and industrial factories, two oddly clashing people spoke in front of a particular building.

"And don't worry—you're just stopping by to introduce yourself today. If you decide you don't like it, you can tell me."

"O-okay."

The tall man was Akabayashi, and the nervous-looking girl standing next to him was Akane Awakusu.

Akane wanted to be stronger.

For the last few days, she'd been through experiences that few grade-schoolers—few adults, in fact—had ever faced. And in this case, she was not the helpless victim, but the agent causing the chaos.

Right after her return a few days ago, she received a tearful embrace from her mother and then got a lecture. But even in the middle of the scolding, she heard the phrase *so glad you're all right* many times, so Akane felt less like she was in trouble and more that she was guilty of inflicting pain.

Yet there was a conflicted feeling inside of her still: Shizuo Heiwajima.

She was attempting to kill a grown man, and yet he had also saved her life. Even she was having difficulty deciphering exactly how she felt about him. While he may have saved her, Akane didn't yet have an answer as to whether she should kill him or not.

It seemed that even this most obvious of questions was beyond her ability to answer.

The world she had known had turned out to be a facade, constructed by fear of the name Awakusu. This was all unbeknownst to her, and when she learned the truth, that facade had crumbled into dust.

The wedge placed there was preventing her from re-creating her world, leaving it—and her—broken. And like a bad drama, that was when she had gotten kidnapped.

On top of that, she had met the impossible Headless Rider on her headless horse, things that shouldn't and couldn't exist in the real world. All these details were enough to melt the pieces of her broken worldview into a sludge.

Things had settled down now, but Akane was still in pieces.

That morning, when Akabayashi visited at her request, the first thing she had said was "How can I get good at killing people?"

The man, an employee of her father's, looked startled at first and then hid his surprise behind a tight smile. "What's this all about? You got it in for somebody?"

"No. It's not that…but I have to kill him."

"…Sounds scary. Who are you talking about?"

"I can't tell you," Akane said, shaking her head.

Akabayashi didn't get angry, nor did he get upset; he just smiled. "Why not?"

"If I say, you guys will go after him, won't you?"

"Is that a bad thing?" he asked matter-of-factly.

Akane nodded. "He's a good person. But I have to kill him."

It wasn't an answer that made a lot of sense, so Akabayashi kept trying to get to the bottom of her reasoning. "Do you want him to die?"

"No. I don't want to kill him."

"...Then why?"

"If I don't kill him, he might kill people I care about..."

"Who told you that?"

"...I'm sorry," she said, her eyes sorrowful. Akabayashi recognized that she wasn't going to be able to tell him the answer, so he approached from a different direction.

"But what if that person is lying to you?"

"...I can't tell."

"But just a moment ago, you said this person you have to kill is good... Are you sure of that?"

"...I can't tell," she repeated. She shook her head, but it wasn't a means of shying away from the question. "I can't tell right now. Everyone, even my friends...my friend's mother...the teacher...Father...*everyone* was lying to me. I don't even know if I can trust you or not..."

"..."

"So I believe that he's good, but now I can't believe myself...so... umm..."

It was clear that the girl did not have it all straight in her heart. She looked down at the ground, as if ready to burst into tears, but the only things that emerged next were words. "But I can't. I have to be stronger."

"Why is that?"

"If it turns out he's bad...and I'm weak, then that's the end of me. I can't just worry about what I should do if he's bad... But I can't talk to Father, either. Because they're all yakuza, right? So he might die before I can even figure out if he's good or bad..."

"This is quite a surprise. Does everyone your age nowadays think about grown-up concepts like this?" Akabayashi asked, impressed. He pondered for a bit, then grinned and said, "Well, I get your point. If you find out he's a bad guy, and you're going to stop him or protect yourself, you've gotta be stronger than him. And at your age... Well, I'd like to believe that us grown-ups aren't impatient enough to kill a guy before figuring out if he deserves it or not..."

He shrugged and suggested, "Here's an idea: Just because you might be up against a killer doesn't mean you have to be stronger than them *at killing*."

"Huh?"

"There's a thing called self-defense. Rather than killing bad guys, it helps you get stronger so that you can protect yourself and the people you care about."

Several hours later, Akane was here in front of this building, with Akabayashi as her escort.

The building had a sign on the front that read TRAUGOTT GEISSEN-DORFER'S RAKUEI GYM, and there was a poster of a tough-looking foreign man hung next to the entrance.

"It makes it sound like he owns or is affiliated with this place, but that Traugott guy actually dabbles in a lot of different fighting styles. What they teach here just so happens to be one of them, so they use that connection as a marketing gimmick. I guess he doesn't mind them using the name, either."

"Ohhh?" Akane replied. She didn't seem to be entirely present. It was less that she failed to understand Akabayashi's explanation and more that she was preoccupied with a great feeling of uneasiness.

An unfamiliar place full of unfamiliar people—these are certainly things that elicit anxiety. But to Akane in particular, there was a fear that even in this new place, she would encounter the same false smiles and words she'd been around all her life. Would they, too, be afraid of the shadow cast by the Awakusu-kai? Would they secretly hate her because of it?

Akane's childhood mind grappled with this very adult apprehension. Her body trembled, and she was about to consider giving up and backing out when she heard an excited girl's voice nearby.

"Ahhh! That Awakusu-kai mobster is abducting a little girl!"

"?!"

The mention of the name Awakusu caused Akane to start. But at the same time, she noticed something odd: The girl's tone of voice was far too cheery for someone bringing up the feared Awakusu name.

She timidly turned around right as Akabayashi said, "Oh really, Mairu? Do I look like that bad of a guy?"

"How can you blame me for thinking that, Mr. Akabayashi? You couldn't look any fishier if you tried!"

"Well, damn." He smirked. The girl cackled.

She had to be about five or six years older than Akane, with braided hair and glasses. While those things might normally suggest a gloomy, withdrawn personality, this girl was lively and bracing. There was a bundle, probably a martial arts outfit, slung over her back, as if she were coming back from a workout.

"As a matter of fact, this girl's name is Akane. She's our chairman's granddaughter."

"Oh! Does that mean she's gonna grow up to be the yakuza lady bossing the guys around?!"

"...! ...!"

Akane was stunned. She assumed she would have to hide her background at the gym, but Akabayashi told the truth to the very first person there. Her mouth trembled in shock, and without a better idea of what to do, she began bopping Akabayashi on the back.

The girl named Mairu took a step closer and helpfully suggested, "Ha-ha! Best plan here would be a sudden attack to the privates!" She unleashed a quick, sharp kick at Akabayashi's groin.

"Yikes!" he mocked, dodging at the last possible moment with a smile. "Man, I've never had *two* girls try to kick me in the balls in the same day before."

"What? Twice? That must mean you made another girl cry this morning. You *are* a bad guy!" Mairu teased with a huge grin. She turned back to Akane and said, "Well, whatever. So you're going to be my junior here! If you pay attention and obey my orders, I'll make you my special henchman and even teach you my signature secret attack, the Thumbtack Special!"

"Cheap barrier of entry for a cheap attack."

"Shut up, Mr. Akabayashi!" she shot back. Mairu was doing all the talking, and Akane hadn't said a word yet. The existence of a person who knew her as the "granddaughter of the Awakusu-kai chairman" and still acted this way was extremely new and surprising to her.

"Well, in any case, you'll be my little-sister fellow pupil, so if there's any problem at all, you come and tell Sis! Here, come with me and I'll introduce you to Master!"

"Great. I've already spoken with the manager, so you can take her through the rest of it. Personally, my recommendation is pole fighting, but I think the fundamentals should come first. Give Akane's dad a call when you're done, and he should send a car to come get her."

"Um, wait, what?"

Akane was unable to wrap her head around how fast things were moving. Akabayashi waved and left, and Akane just watched him go as Mairu dragged her inside the building.

On the inside, a little flame kindled at the excitement of things taking an unexpected course.

♂♀

Ikebukuro, apartment building

"...Can't imagine what the boss is thinking, agreeing to this," Tom grumbled as he climbed the rickety, old apartment stairs.

As usual, the person they were about to meet on the fourth floor of this particular building had abandoned his tab, and they were heading to collect from him—but unlike normal, there was another assistant in addition to Shizuo.

"I submit a doubt. I have not heard the contents of the job our group is performing," said the white woman named Vorona, in her usual strange Japanese.

The chef at Russia Sushi had said she was too unfriendly to work in the service industry and asked them to take her for their job, as long as he called their boss. So here she was.

I figured he meant that she would go and do office work for him... Instead, she's collecting with us?!

The only way Tom could imagine a woman collecting debt was if she was a landlord or the manager of a bar—the thought of traveling around with a woman as a coworker was one he had never entertained.

Vorona had changed from her uniform into plainclothes, and he had to admit that her figure had been accentuated by the change in a most bewitching way.

Damn... Yeah, it sounds nice working with a hot chick, until you actually have to do it...

In this case, the woman was supremely standoffish and seemed acutely disinterested in men. Tom answered her question by saying, "We're collecting money from bad people who owe it and aren't paying up. Got that?"

He tried to make it as simple as possible, since her Japanese was questionable at best. Vorona nodded to indicate understanding and said, "Collection of protection money. Roger."

"No, no, it's not protection money... You know what, never mind."

Seriously, I'm not sure about this.

Would they fail to be taken seriously if there was a woman with them? Tom wondered. It wasn't his intention to belittle women, but there was no guarantee that the targets they were going to collect from would feel the same way.

Actually, they could belittle all they wanted, but if that disrespect extended to Shizuo, and he got carried away and killed someone—well, that was the worst possible outcome.

Also, I feel like this babe keeps staring him down. Is that just my imagination?

As for Shizuo, he'd been traveling along in silence with his arms folded, apparently deep in thought. Perhaps he himself was trying to figure out what he might have done to deserve all the staring.

Just then, Tom reached the target's apartment. He tried ringing the bell for starters and immediately heard the lock opening from within.

When the door opened, it revealed a man with an old-fashioned "punch perm" of the kind tough guys wore in the '80s.

"...Who the hell are you?"

"I'm guessing you'll understand if we say we're here on behalf of the dating site Arachne?" Tom said by way of introduction. The permed man's face froze for a moment.

"...! No idea what you mean."

"Yeah, yeah, I'm sure. But your phone number has already used one hundred seventy thousand yen worth of services. It's all in the contract, so the normal legal channel would involve having the lawyer collect, but neither of us wants to get the court involved, do we?"

"Shuddup! Quit talkin' yer mumbo jumbo, or I'll kill you!"

"If you found that explanation to be 'mumbo jumbo,' then we might need to bring in an interpreter," Tom suggested, annoyed. The permed man found this amusing; he wore a crude smile.

"Sure thing...I got an interpreter."

"What?"

"C'mon, boys!" the man shouted toward the interior of the apartment.

A number of men marched up to the doorway. They all had the appearance of tried-and-true low-class thugs, and they filed out to face Tom's group in the hallway of the building. Years of experience and intuition told Tom that they were just ruffians, not professional criminals.

Triumphantly, the man with the perm returned to Tom and gloated, "What did you want interpreted? Were you gonna hand over that chick to us, maybe?"

Good grief, Tom thought. *Normally, Shizuo would just snap and be done with it, but since we have Vorona with us today, I guess we should back down.*

He turned toward the young woman. *And if they won't let us walk away, we'll at least have to make sure she gets a...way...? Huh?*

Vorona had been standing right behind Shizuo just a moment ago, but now she was gone.

"Huh? Whaddaya want, ba...*buh?!*"

He suddenly screamed.

Huh? Tom spun around to face forward again, and in the process, he noticed that Shizuo's eyes were bulging. When his spin finished, Tom's eyes bulged, too.

"Wha—?!" "Hey...you...ah!" "Hrg?!" "Whoa?!"

He saw the men groaning and collapsing, as Vorona spun and moved between all of them. It was like an action scene in a movie.

Vorona's moves were just as flashy and brilliant as her appearance. She flowed from target to target, striking the men in the chins and throats with her elbows and toes, knocking them unconscious one after the other.

Once they were down and immobile, she started going through their pockets. Soon she was handing Tom a small pile of wallets. Sadly, the Japanese language of her statement was a far cry from the smooth, practiced action moves.

"Please teach the precise amount of money to be deducted. If it is lacking, shall we conduct a home search?"

♂♀

Even then, at the very moment that Tom and Shizuo shared a glance...
...the rumors raced through the town.

"Hey, you see that?"

"Shizuo."   "That was Shizuo Heiwajima."   "With a woman."

"Was that injury story made up?"   "No idea."

"There was definitely a woman."   "Maybe she's with the dreads guy?"

"Nah, I saw them in town."   "She was hot."

"And the whole time they were walking...she was staring at Shizuo."

♂♀

Several hours later, Ikebukuro, Kishimojin Temple

"I can't believe I wasn't expecting something like that, knowing that she was connected to Simon and that sushi chef," Tom lamented.

They had visited a number of other targets after that, and every one of them had either tried to hit on Vorona or threatened the group—with the result that Vorona knocked them out so quickly and handily that Shizuo didn't even have time to get angry once.

"Try to spare a thought for the guys who have to mop all this up..."

"Mop up? Do you mean to dispose of the dead bodies? I have heard the standard method of Japan is sinking into Tokyo Bay."

"No, there's no standard of the sort. Can you try to explain this to her, Shizuo?"

"...I'm not really in a position to say, actually," he replied.

They came to a temple for revering Kishimojin, a Buddhist goddess of protection. It was on the route from a Toden trolley stop toward Ikebukuro Station. Their next job was close by, but they decided to stop here at the Kishimojin Temple and take a breather.

It was a quiet location in the middle of a residential area, with countless trees in the expansive temple grounds, their leaves catching and splitting the reddening light of the sun—an oasis of tranquillity in the midst of the vast, bustling metropolis.

The trio, however, was in a very strange mood when it decided to stop for a break. For his part, Tom was silent as he tried to think of how he should broach the topic at hand—but to his surprise, it was Shizuo who broke the ice with Vorona.

"You seem like you're pretty tough. You practice some kind of fighting?"

"..."

She stared at him, clearly conflicted. Whatever emotional knot was behind the look on her face was completely beyond Tom's understanding.

After a long silence, Vorona sighed heavily and said, "I have learned only the first of first steps in many things. In youth period, through texts. In puberty, through battle. Denis and Semyon...the one you call Simon, taught me self-defense."

"Ahh, those guys... So if you started in childhood, does that mean your dad was a fighter, too?"

"My father was expert in a fighting style called Systema. Systema was the only style I did not learn. It is...similar to rebellion against Father. I would appreciate if you do not pry."

"I won't ask, then. In any case, you're pretty incredible."

"...It sounds like farcical jest coming from you," Vorona insisted.

Tom jumped in. "Huh...? Wait, do you know about Shizuo?"

"In Ikebukuro, it is impossible not to hear rumors," she lied. She had only learned of Shizuo's prowess once she saw him in action the day before. But because she'd been wearing a helmet and they hardly spoke, Shizuo did not realize it was her yet.

Perhaps Vorona had heard a rumor or two about a man wearing a bartender's outfit. But she would have laughed off stories about throwing vending machines one-handed as a joke.

After yesterday, she had experienced his strength firsthand.

Perhaps this man, she contemplated, recalling that moment and the sight of him kicking a car like a ball and overturning everything she thought she knew. *Perhaps this man could prove it to me, I hoped. Perhaps he could give me the answer to the question of humanity's frailty.*

But the excitement of that moment had totally fizzled into nothing overnight.

It was me who was unfit all along. I am…weak. What is the point of striking a block of clay to determine how strong steel is? All this means is that the people I destroyed to get here…were weaker than clay.

This was total nonsense, of course, but Vorona had settled into another glare at Shizuo. She didn't hate him. The fierceness in her eyes was actually directed at herself.

For his part, Shizuo didn't realize he was being stared at. He gazed up at the sky over the temple and murmured, "I dunno what rumors you heard about me, but I think you're more incredible than I am."

"…It is unclear what you are saying."

"I just happen to have physical strength. That has nothing to do with whether a person is really *strong* or *weak*. If anything, the folks like you, who worked and worked to train themselves, are way stronger people than I am. That's worthy of respect."

"…"

I am more incredible than him? What is he saying? Maybe I just misheard him, Vorona thought.

Tom spoke up to fill the silence. "That reminds me—you said there was some fighter you respected. What was the name again…?"

"Traugott Geissendorfer. He's unbelievable."

"See, that's crazy to me. From my perspective, you're the most ridiculous of all, Shizuo. If you wanted to, you could easily bulk up and win gold medals. And once you get a bunch of them… Wait, are the medals pure gold?" Tom wondered.

"Gold medals used in Olympics are not all pure gold. Consideration for host countries with poor economy. Over ninety-two-point-five percent pure silver with six-gram coating of gold. Only pure gold medals are Nobel Prize until 1980. Even modern Nobel medal is seventy-five percent gold with pure gold coat," Vorona answered.

She'd meant it to distract from the previous topic, and it succeeded in surprising Tom. "Wow...I feel like I just saw another incredible side of you."

"How come they stopped using all gold for the Nobel Prize? They didn't have the money?" Shizuo asked. His curiosity reminded Vorona of Slon and briefly rattled her heart, but her instincts took over and produced the answer from memory.

"Nobel award has cash prize. But medal of pure gold is too soft. A simple bite leaves a mark. Even little accidents cause string of marks, distortions. Alloys prevent disfiguration."

"Oooh, I didn't know that..."

"Tough, smart, and beautiful. You've got everything," Tom remarked, but it did not please Vorona.

"...Denied. I am not beautiful, smart, and certainly not—" she started to say, words intended to convince herself, but she paused partway. There was a girl near the entrance of the temple grounds, shouting with innocent excitement.

"Ohhh! Shiii-zuuu-ooo! How are youuu?"

The trio turned and saw a girl with braided hair and glasses, a rolled-up dojo *gi* slung over her back. Behind her was another girl who looked identical to her except for a gloomy expression, and then a little girl who was clearly several years younger than them.

Shizuo recognized them all. "Is that Mairu and Kururi...and Akane?!"

The little elementary-age girl hiding behind the twins saw Shizuo and trotted forward at a run.

"Big Brother Shizuo!"

♂♀

"Hey, it's me. Listen up."

"The rumor was true!"   "I was just watching Shizuo from afar!"

"This little girl ran over to Shizuo and just straight up hugged him!"

"Really?"   "Shizuo's kid?"

"So not only was the woman part true, so was the kid!"

The rumor raced through a specific class of people like a thunderbolt.

Cell phones and the Internet acted as a medium, giving shape to the rumor in real time—and provided these rumormongers with almost pathological excitement.

"How many people can we get here right away...?"

The rumor that was more wishful thinking than logic turned out to be true.

Of course, in reality it wasn't true at all, but they were now convinced of its accuracy, anyway.

And that was because they needed it to be true, which meant that considering any other possibility was pointless.

Excitement overtook the gossiping gaggle's bodies, gifting them with a dynamic agency they could never exhibit otherwise—no matter what their goals were.

"I dunno what's gonna happen, but I want at least a dozen guys in some cars."

"Once the girls leave Shizuo's side, we're gonna kidnap 'em."

♂♀

Why is Akane Awakusu here?

Vorona quietly scanned the area, surprised. She suspected that some of the Awakusu-kai were nearby.

I'm wasting my time, she realized. They could certainly be watching her now, but they would not do so from out in the open where she would see. And without any gear on her person, she would be helpless if anyone on the level of that Akabayashi man showed up.

No, wait… We already settled the matter. As long as I do not touch that Akane girl, the Awakusu-kai will not harass me. On the other hand, I don't know how sincere they are about that deal, so there's nothing wrong with being cautious.

In any case…I will not rest easy within the security Father bought for me.

Meanwhile, the three girls chattered and squealed, though the majority of the noise was coming from the one with glasses.

"Hey! Hey! Who's that pretty lady?! Can I hug her?!"

"Don't do it," said Shizuo, grabbing the girl by the back of her collar and holding her aloft like a cat.

The other one, wearing a gloomy face, bowed to Tom. "…Earlier… bag…thanks…" [Thank you for the bag to hide the money the other day.]

"Oh, sure. Don't mention it," he replied.

"And since we got another three hundred thousand this morning, we were able to carry it around in that bag, Kuru!"

"Three hun—!" Tom gasped. He decided to tap the girls on the shoulders and advised, "Listen…this isn't really my place to say, but… don't do anything that would disappoint your parents. You're such sweet kids—you shouldn't sell yourselves short like this. I mean, three hundred thousand yen is a lot of cash, but it's an asset you shouldn't put a price on…"

"?" "?"

The twins looked confused. Tom's lecture was based on an entirely mistaken assumption.

Akane, meanwhile, clung to Shizuo's pants as she looked up at him with a beaming smile. "Thanks for yesterday, Big Brother Shizuo!"

"Hmm? Oh, sure, don't mention it. Kids like you oughta be more free-spirited; don't go dragging your obligations around with you," he said with a grimace and stroked her head. Akane squealed and pressed his hand down with her own.

Seeing this, Vorona thought, *She is so carefree. Especially for having been abducted by us just yesterday. Or…perhaps it's actually a sign of strength that she's already overcome her hardship. I suppose I really am weaker than anyone...*

Next, Shizuo addressed the twins: "So what are you two doing with Akane, anyway?"

"We're more surprised that *you* know Akane, Shizuo! Turns out that she just joined my dojo today! My training for the day is over, so once Kuru came by, I decided to give Akane a tour of the area!"

"Oh, your dojo? So it's for self-defense? Not a bad idea, actually," Shizuo replied.

"D-do you think so? Then I'll give it a shot," Akane said, smiling.

Shizuo's grin faded a bit as he considered something. He turned back to the twins. "Speaking of which...what's up with your fleabrain brother?"

"...Surprise...?" [Huh...?]

"Don't you watch the news on TV, Shizuo?"

"What? Well, I left early to do the collection rounds. Why? Was there something interesting on the news? Did they finally arrest him?"

"It's a secret. You should check the papers or the Internet when you get back home. You'll be amazed!"

"...Brother...safe..." [Izaya escaped with his life.]

"?"

Shizuo wasn't sure what she meant by that and was going to ask for more information when Tom cut him off: "Hey, Shizuo, we gotta go hit up that place already."

"Right," he grunted, switching back to work mode.

"This place will be a little delicate, as there's a family involved, Vorona. Do you mind waiting this one out?" Tom continued.

"...I am on standby?"

"Well, we don't want you putting on a big display like the last few. Why don't you just stay here with these girls and chat over some tea? Uh, tea not included."

Tom Tanaka's best quality was his ability to adjust to any person's needs. Once he got used to them, he could adapt and learn to get along with anyone, even people like Shizuo and Vorona, who normal folks would instantly be too afraid to approach.

One of Tom's on-the-fly adjustments was recognizing that Vorona, who was more suited to action and not negotiation, was best left behind on this one. Of course, he was still going to bring along Shizuo as a valuable means of ensuring his own safety.

"Well," he decided, "it's a good thing we've got so many girls here to keep you company. Shizuo and I should be back in, oh, about ten minutes. You can wait alone if you really want, but I'd hate for you to feel lonely on your first day at the job. Can I ask you girls to hang out here?"

"Sure."

"...Pleasure..." [I'd be happy to.]

"I'll wait here until you come back, Big Brother Shizuo!"

With those approvals in place, the four women decided to remain on the temple grounds.

None of them realized that they were being watched.

♂♀

"Hey, Shizuo just split off from the girls! You ready yet?!"

"Don't worry. It'll be less than a minute."

"Also, I doubt they mean anything, but...there are also two teenage girls there who seem to know him."

"So we'll grab them, too."

"Really? All of them? You sure, man?"

"Well, the rumor I heard is..."

"Yesterday, the Dollars abducted a group of, like, five girls, including some motorcycle gang boss's lady."

♂♀

Several minutes later

"Ohhh, you know Simon? So does that mean you know Egor, too?!"

"...It is a surprise. It is outside of expectations that you would recognize Egor."

"...Surprise...strange..." [This is quite a coincidence.]

Vorona and the girls found it no trouble at all to keep up a conversation after Tom and Shizuo left. She had assumed there would be a long

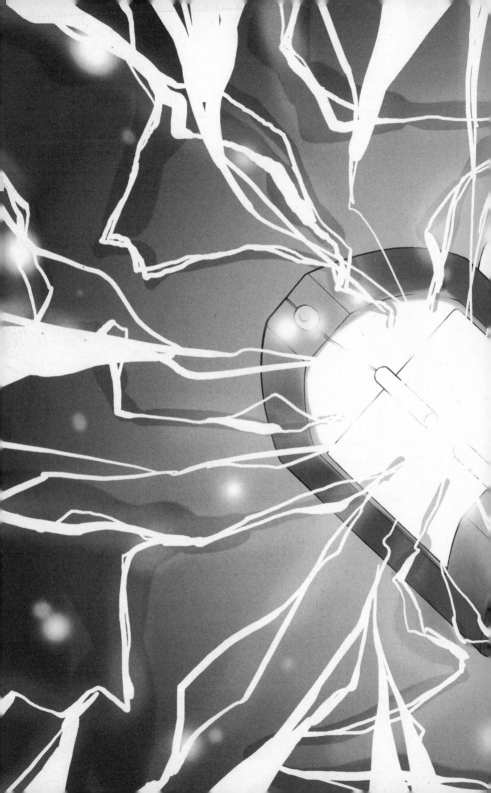

silence with nothing to talk about, but the girl with the braids and her gloomy identical companion weren't intimidated by her in the least.

To everyone's surprise, they found they had some strange things in common. Vorona decided to obey her new boss's orders and stay there so she could continue the conversation.

But what should I do after this...? I'm much closer now to the man in the bartender clothes, which is good. I know his name. But what now? Do I wait for my chance and attack him from behind? But...why?

Even the nature of the hope she clung to was beginning to evade Vorona. Suddenly, Akane tugged at her sleeve.

"...Are you a friend of Big Brother Shizuo?"

"Huh?"

It was the very girl she kidnapped the day before. Apparently, the girl did not recognize her. For her part, Vorona considered the girl to be merely an element of a past event and not worthy of any personal sentiment.

"...Friend...? Rejected. Shizuo and I are nothing but work companions."

"Oh, I see," Akane said, looking relieved for a reason that evaded Vorona.

But it didn't matter, because in the next moment, the Russian woman detected an anomaly in the area.

A number of cars stopped on the adjacent street and opened their doors, almost entirely at once.

—!

Alarms went off in Vorona's head. She crouched immediately and glanced around the temple grounds.

Emerging from several nearby vans was a group of men wearing ski masks, like bank robbers did. They didn't have any visible weapons, but they did seem to be carrying ropes and sacks.

"Huh? What? What's this? That doesn't look good!"

"...Bad...?" [Kidnappers?]

Sure enough, the men were on a beeline right toward them. They were racing at full speed, their sacks rustling with a violence that would be menacing to an ordinary person.

But that was the key part: to an ordinary person.

*　　*　　*

They would spread out in a circle around the girls and put the sacks over their heads. Once the girls were blinded and panicking, they'd load them into the cars and drive off.

Very simple job.

But not an easy one.

The area happened to be empty at the moment, but a resident might pass by at any time. In order to minimize the risk of being witnessed, the men were going to have to be rough, if necessary. All they had to do was pull off this job, and then they could use or destroy the weapon that was Shizuo Heiwajima in any way they desired.

However, they certainly didn't imagine that the women who were with Shizuo also happened to be deadly weapons, when handled improperly.

The white woman looked like the biggest and strongest of the group.

The man who attempted to throw his sack over her head was the first to taste the weapon's bite.

"…You seek to target me?"

Vorona let out a short breath, leaped off the ground—and aimed her right foot squarely at the jaw of the man, with all the torque of a chameleon's tongue flicking out. Her steel-plated boot passed right through his upheld arms, the high kick smooth and flowing.

Her toe connected with his chin with pinpoint accuracy. The man's eyes rolled back into his head, and he passed out, unaware of what had actually happened to him.

"…Huh?"

The men who witnessed this action experienced a temporary mental fog, a void of experience. It was not fear at Vorona's strength—it was simple lack of understanding of what they'd just seen.

But when the mind stops, the body often does not.

The men raced toward their targets, temporarily careless and preoccupied, only to receive a very painful counterattack—not just from Vorona, but all the girls.

"Goddammit, stop stru…*gah!*"

Mairu jabbed her fingers in the eyes of the man trying to hold her down. She didn't crush the eyeballs, but it was enough to make him leap backward. She then used those extended fingers to grab his ski mask so that he yanked his head free as he pulled away. With his face exposed, she swung her hands forward to slap him right on the ears—the kind of dangerous, precise strike meant to rupture the eardrums.

One of the other men automatically looked over when he heard the sound of his companion screaming and rolling on the ground. That was enough time for Kururi to pull a spray can out of her pocket and deploy it.

It was a small can, like a purse-sized perfume bottle. It contained a self-defense substance of her own design, based on store-bought mace.

The reason it was only *based* on the common market product was so that it could be several times more powerful.

"Wha...wha...?!"

The largest of the attackers, seeing that his buddies were going down left and right, finally noticed that something was wrong.

"Dammit, screw this crap!" he ranted, grabbing the nearest girl, the slow-looking one with the spray can, so that he could subdue her through brute force. But because he was so tall, he failed to notice the youngest girl approaching his feet.

"...What?"

There was a brief crackle, and he looked down to see—

"Y-yah!"

Akane Awakusu hit him right on the leg with her stun gun.

She'd gotten the gun from Nakura the other day as a means to kill Shizuo. Fortunately for the man—and Akane—Shinra had modified the device while Akane was sleeping to ensure it wouldn't be fatal.

Of course, nonfatal is not the same thing as nondebilitating.

Froth bubbled out the man's mouth and nose before he could even scream. Akane switched the stun gun off immediately and hid behind Mairu.

Why does she have a stun gun? Vorona wondered. *Well...after what just happened to her, I suppose she was given one for protection. But she seems very adept with it...*

Vorona pondered this question as she knocked out the men one after the other. At first, she assumed that this was a hit squad sent by someone seeking revenge against her or perhaps some new group of kidnappers to abduct Akane Awakusu after she had failed.

"Sh-shit! What's up with these bitches?!" the men wailed in panic.

"Who said kidnapping them would work against Shizuo? Whose bright idea was this?!"

At this, Vorona suddenly understood.

Aha... We're supposed to be hostages against Shizuo... They wanted to take down Shizuo Heiwajima.

She suddenly realized she was smiling. *Don't make me laugh.*

A man lunged for her from the side, and she stomped her heel hard onto the top of his foot. When he grunted and lurched forward, she spun and slammed her knee into the bridge of his nose.

You think you...are capable of toppling him?

Recall.

Recall.

Those who you destroyed in the past.

These men here are nothing but soft putty, a far cry from even those old victims.

But as she knocked them out left and right with her bare hands, Vorona began to recall other things.

Her own nature, forgotten after consecutive defeats.

Her pathological urges that she could not control.

It's not enough. These men are not enough. Humanity is...not this frail. Shizuo Heiwajima...is not this frail!

The urge to destroy, which had given her so much pleasure, came to her under the guise of finding out if humanity really was a frail thing. But that urge, which meant nothing more to her than an excuse to kill for pleasure, was now changing in subtle ways.

Strong... I want to be strong.

Strong like that man, harder than diamond and vaster than the tundra forests! If I can destroy Shizuo Heiwajima, then perhaps...I can gain fulfillment I shall never find elsewhere.

These thoughts roared through her mind as she kicked, struck, toppled, and overwhelmed the men—a forced smile plastered across her face.

She told herself that it would only be a true smile when she defeated Shizuo.

"Uh, cr-crap! Let's pull back!"

The men fled in panic, totally unprepared for the resistance they received. They raced for their vans, but one of them was already pulling away.

"H-hey, you idiot! Wait, don't lea..."

But once they got to the street, they realized why the car took off. From the other end of the street, two men with distinctive appearances were approaching—one in a bartender outfit, the other with dreads.

"I-it's...Shizuo!"

"Quick, get in!"

They piled into the remaining car as if they were fleeing from some horrifying dinosaur, some of them even hanging off the door handles as it pulled away.

Tom watched in confusion as the cars full of screaming men departed. "What the hell was that all about? Did they have a fight?"

Shizuo glanced toward the temple, saw that Akane and the other women were all standing around normally, then shook his head and remarked, "Fighting right in front of the goddess Kishimojin. Have they no shame?"

As a matter of fact, the men had been attempting something far worse than a simple fight; fortunately, their plot ended in spectacular failure.

The men raced off out of sight, too terrified to consider their good fortune that they were not spotted in the act by Shizuo.

♂♀

"...There was a mistake in my answer to your prior question," Vorona murmured as the man in the bartender getup approached. She was back to her usual stony expression, and her voice was so quiet that only Akane heard her.

"Huh...?" the girl said, confused.

Vorona didn't bother to stay quiet. She came right out and said, "Shizuo Heiwajima. He is my prey. Eventually, I will destroy him. That is truth."

"...! N-no! You can't!" Akane pleaded. She tugged on Vorona's trousers. "*I'm* going to beat Big Brother Shizuo!"

Young as she was, even Akane couldn't have described exactly what emotion it was that had just risen within her heart. She simply heard Vorona say that she would destroy Shizuo, and that complex interplay of emotions delivered a single answer to her.

I need to kill Big Brother Shizuo. But I don't want to... Umm, umm...

She wasn't able to find a way to rephrase her words, so all she could come up with was a vague follow-up.

"I have to do something about Big Brother Shizuo!"

"...Answer is unclear. Please provide reason that you hold ownership of my prey."

"I...I don't know all that complicated stuff!" Akane argued back. Meanwhile, Mairu and Kururi simply watched the argument, wide-eyed. It was just then that Tom showed up.

"Huh? Where's Shizuo?" Mairu asked.

Tom gestured over his shoulder with his chin.

"Just getting a can of coffee from the vending machine back there," he said before noticing the argument going on. "Hey, what's...?"

"Shizuo is mine."

"No! You can't touch Big Brother Shizuo!"

"............? ...?!"

Huh?!

This development was so abrupt and absurd that Tom's eyes grew to the size of golf balls behind his glasses.

W-wait...what?! What's going on here?! When did the situation turn into...this?!

Meanwhile, Shizuo finished up his coffee and reentered the temple grounds.

"Big Brother Shizuo!"

"Hey. Have you been getting along with them?" he asked Akane, rubbing her head. She turned and glared daggers back at Vorona.

Shizuo never saw the fireworks going off between them.

♂♀

"Dammit! What the hell was that? Who were those chicks?!" one of the thugs ranted back at their hideout, yanking his ski mask off.

They were the remnants of a street gang crushed by Shizuo in the past. The few that remained back at the base rushed up to see what happened.

"What do you mean? You guys failed?!"

"Well, I guess I see why she's Shizuo's woman... Damn it all!"

"I wouldn't worry too much. We can wait for that kid with the stun gun to start walking alone and nab her then."

"Yeah, we left a few back there to keep an eye out. As long as they keep watching, the chicks'll definitely split up, so we can get them one by one," one of the returning men bragged. He hadn't learned his lesson yet.

Of course, these were guys who'd been beaten by Shizuo once and were actually going for a second attempt—learning wasn't their strong suit.

In this particular case, they weren't going to get a second attempt.

"Are *these* your lookouts?"

There were some dull, heavy thuds at the entrance, where two large lumps of flesh were now placed. The men were unconscious, their faces red and swollen.

Then the people who brought them back to that pummeled state entered the hideout.

"What?! Who the...fu...?"

They were very menacing figures, over ten in total. These men wore a variety of outfits—black suits, sweat suits, work clothes—but all of them contained that air of deadly seriousness that marked them as being of a *professional* nature.

"Who was it you said you were going to kidnap?"

"Er, uh..."

"Going after Miss Akane, of all people? Did y'all want to be metal men that bad? Should we go take a trip to the smelting tank and see what happens?"

"Eh…? Eh…?!"

These men were all part of the Awakusu-kai.

Some members who had been secretly keeping watch over Akane saw that she was making contact with Vorona and called for backup—then the gang attacked and was promptly beaten, only for a few of them to return to the scene as lookouts.

The Awakusu men subdued them without drawing Akane's attention and worked the location of the hideout out of the hapless lookouts. Naturally, the thugs had no idea who Akane was or what she represented, so this was all a terrifying mystery to them.

"Wait…! Hang on, we don't know… We were just… Shizuo?"

"Save your breath. We can hear all the details back at the office. Get your story straight now while you have the chance."

"W-wait, no…"

"See, if your story is bad, then the next step is coming up with your last will and testament—not that we're actually going to pass it on."

The Awakusu-kai men got right to work with clinical precision. Given that they were merely taking some punks who got beat up by a group of girls back to the office, it was a very, very easy job indeed—one they conducted without mercy.

And that was how rumor and hearsay contributed to the downfall of one particular gang.

♂♀

Ikebukuro

Akane and the twins left, so the debt-collecting trio headed off to its next job.

Tom kept glancing toward Shizuo as they walked, occasionally offering a cryptic comment.

"…Well, given who your brother is, I guess you've got the looks…"

"What's up, Tom? You've been acting weird."

"Nah…it's nothing. Ignore me."

"?"

Shizuo was still curious, but he gave up asking Tom. Instead, he turned around to Vorona.

"By the way, Vorona…"

"What is it?"

"Have you and I met somewhere before?"

"…?!"

Did he figure it out? Vorona wondered, instantly tense.

She'd had her face covered, and the only words she'd said to him were "Motorbike is mine."

The bike in question had been destroyed, and there was a firefight following that, but she'd been in her riding suit and full helmet the entire time, so he hadn't seen her face. Still, a perceptive person might have noticed.

She decided to take great care with her answer. "It is secret. Do you mind that I wish to refuse the answer?"

"…"

Shizuo didn't reply. He walked over to a nearby vending machine and bought a can of coffee. It seemed strange, since he'd just had one a moment earlier—but this one he gave to Vorona.

"?"

"It's on me."

"…"

"See…before now, I bounced around between a lot of jobs… It's the first time I've ever had a junior coworker to mentor," Shizuo said with a grin. "Tell you what, I'll let go of the fine details. You seemed like you were getting along with Akane, and if Simon introduced you to us, I'm sure you're a good person."

"…"

It's like he's a completely different person from when he kicked that car. And I still can't tell if he realizes who I am or not.

"Well, here's to a good working relationship," Shizuo said and pressed the can of coffee against Vorona's cheek. It squashed the flesh out of shape, but her expression was still as blank as ever.

"…Fwank you."

Shizuo Heiwajima… What a strange man.

As far as she knew, he was the toughest human alive. Yet she still knew nothing about him.

Over time, I shall learn more and more. And once I know everything, I will destroy him. That is my reason for living, Vorona decided and drank the coffee.

It tasted rich and dark, with just a little bit of sugar. Oddly, it seemed rather sweet to her.

Vorona turned to Shizuo, face as impassive as ever.

"…Thank you…sir."

♂♀

"H-hey, did you hear?!"

"The guys going after Shizuo got nabbed by the Awakusu-kai."

"For real?"   "How come?!"   "Guess his bird's an Awakusu relative."

"What does that mean?"   "Is Shizuo the Awakusu-kai heir?"

The absurd rumors circled all over Ikebukuro, changing constantly.

"You hear? Did you hear, man?!"

"Shizuo's the secret love child of the Awakusu-kai chairman?!"
"Whoa, really?!"

"Yeah, with a Russian woman!"   "So that's why Shizuo's blond!"

"I thought that was hair dye?   "Crazy!"   "Okay, don't mess with him."

"I'm not scared!"   "But who wants to make an enemy of the Awakusu-kai?"

*   *   *

And once the rumors got truly absurd, those half-hearted ruffians immediately believed in them.

They had no choice. They had to believe them. Many wished it to be true with all their heart.

I really, really don't want to have to deal with a monster like Shizuo.

This wasn't the hope that they might actually beat him—it was even more powerful, something like basic animal instinct.

So they clung to the rumors. As long as the rumors were true, they had a valid reason to fear Shizuo. Where before they could not shy away from one man and retain their pride, the presence of the Awakusu-kai backbone gave them a proper rationale for not attacking the individual in question.

And that secret desire of theirs gave birth to more rumors.

Several months later, a third-rate tabloid took the story seriously and wrote an article proclaiming, "Yuuhei Hanejima's Grandfather: Yakuza Boss?!" Not only did they get into trouble with his talent agency, it also attracted the attention of the Awakusu-kai, nearly putting the publisher into bankruptcy.

But that's another story.

New rumors were born every day, racing through Ikebukuro—to serve as a bridge between the ordinary and extraordinary, between people and city.

"Hey... Did you hear?"

Ordinary D Lovey-Dovey Chaka-Poko

Chaka-poko, chaka-poko.

The carriage trundled along behind the horse.

The silhouette suggested a relaxed, regal air as it glided through the light and shade of the trees, as elegant as a leaf drifting through the vast expanse of time.

All except for one detail...

The silhouette of the carriage was indeed nothing but a silhouette.

It was black without reflection, the very absence of light. A carriage somehow expanded from a two-dimensional plane of shadow into a three-dimensional object.

It was the kind of carriage that nobles would have traveled in not too long ago, but in this situation, it was like an illustration taken from a children's book—a pop-up shadow-play children's book, perhaps.

If anything added to the strangely alien nature of the sight, it was the horse pulling it, which wore a Western-style horse helmet that, like the rest of the carriage, was pitch-black and nonreflective.

Seen through the window of this shadow-play carriage come to life were two figures that couldn't have been more different.

One was a young man wearing a white coat that stood in stark contrast to the carriage. The other was dressed in a manner befitting the vehicle's owner—black clothes that seemed to be made of shadow itself.

The woman in black took out a PDA and showed it to the man.

"It's the first time I've tried making a roofed carriage. I guess I can do it, after all," the screen read.

The man in white beamed immensely. "Of course. Nothing is impossible for you, Celty."

"It's hard to take that as a compliment, because you say that sort of thing to me all the time."

"Unfair! Fine, Celty—I shall challenge the limits of human possibility if that's what will serve as proof of your hard work. Just give the order: What must I do? I could write a thousand pages of poems about your beloved Ikebukuro and print more copies of them worldwide than the Bible!" he babbled. The woman in black just typed into the PDA in silence.

"Shinra."

"Mhm?!"

"Shut up for a bit."

"...Mm."

The man named Shinra sulked like a scolded child. The woman named Celty shrugged and jabbed at him with an elbow.

"Don't get so depressed. All the highs and lows are too much to deal with."

"...But you can't blame me for being excited!" Shinra said, his eyes sparkling again. "We haven't gone on a vacation together since I was a kid and you let me ride on the back of the motorcycle!"

"Does that count as a vacation?"

"Well, if you don't think of that as a vacation, that makes this our very first! It's incredible—what a historic day! Should I think of this as a honeymoon?!"

"Be careful to behave—unless you want one of those posthoneymoon 'Oops, I've made a mistake' divorces."

"Yes, ma'am," Shinra grumbled, all good behavior. His shoulders slumped, and he looked down—then leaped up off his seat, looking as if a lightning bolt struck his mind, shouting, "Y-you didn't deny that this was our honeym— *Gahk!*"

The carriage jolted, and he slammed his head on the interior ceiling.

"A-are you all right?!"

"Owww... I'm fine... Just saw stars for a moment..."

"Are you sure you're all right? Sorry, maybe I set the ceiling a bit low. I'm not wearing my helmet, so my sense of height is a bit off," Celty typed into her PDA. She rubbed his head tenderly.

"No, it's fine. It's just the right height. It was my fault for jumping up like that."

"No, I mean, are you sure you're all right? I don't really have a good gauge on how much it hurts to hit your head…"

"It's fine, it's fine. You're better off not knowing. Also, that was the third time you asked me if I was all right. Your kindness is the most effective ice pack of all, Celty."

"Don't be stupid," she typed and then turned toward the window.

Oh, Celty, Shinra thought. *She must have red cheeks right about now. What a sweetheart.*

As a matter of fact, he had no way of knowing if her cheeks were really blushing.

She didn't have cheeks to flush in the first place.

♂♀

Celty Sturluson was not human.

She was a type of fairy commonly known as a dullahan, found from Scotland to Ireland—a being that visits the homes of those close to death to inform them of their impending mortality.

The dullahan carried its own severed head under its arm, rode on a two-wheeled carriage called a Coiste Bodhar pulled by a headless horse, and approached the homes of the soon to die. Anyone foolish enough to open the door was drenched with a basin full of blood. Thus the dullahan, like the banshee, made its name as a herald of ill fortune throughout European folklore.

One theory claimed that the dullahan bore a strong resemblance to the Norse Valkyrie, but Celty had no way of knowing if this was true.

It wasn't that she didn't know; more accurately, she just couldn't remember.

When someone back in her homeland had stolen her head, she had lost all her memories of what she was. It was the search for the faint trail of her head that had brought her here to Ikebukuro.

Now with a motorcycle instead of a headless horse and a riding suit instead of armor, she had wandered the streets of this neighborhood for decades.

But ultimately, she had not succeeded at retrieving her head, and her memories were still lost.

Celty, however, knew who had stolen her head originally.

She also knew who was preventing her from finding it.

But ultimately, that meant she didn't know where it was.

And she was fine with that.

As long as she could be with those human beings she loved and who accepted her, she could happily live the way she was now.

She was a headless woman who let her actions speak for her missing face, who held the strong, secret desire to live within her heart.

That was Celty Sturluson in a nutshell.

But even for the very embodiment of the unusual and extraordinary, Celty had her own flavor of ordinary life.

She was a courier in Ikebukuro, taking various kinds of cargo to designated locations for money. Some people treated her like an odd-jobs guy who could do anything you needed, but she considered all of it to be a part-time job. She was not a professional.

Until about a year ago, she figured that if she did this job and traveled all over every inch of Ikebukuro, she might increase her chances of finding her head—but at this point, her dedication to the job was more rooted in just feeling guilty about the people who wouldn't receive their important items otherwise.

In the past, she took on jobs that might have skirted the law, but now she did her best to avoid things of that nature. It was one thing if *she* got chased by the police or criminal organizations, but now she had people to care for—people she didn't want harmed by this trouble.

On the other hand, Shinra Kishitani—the person she cared for first and foremost—was a black market doctor, an occupation designed to attract trouble.

Celty was essentially honest and caring by nature. She took her job seriously and even went out of her way to help people on her days off. She kept herself busy. On the days when she really was at leisure, she played games with Shinra and relaxed around the house—essentially the same things she did after she got home, anyway.

*   *   *

So in that sense, today's vacation was an actual holiday for her, a real break from tradition.

They were in the mountains, far from the city.

Just a carriage trundling along on a path with a view of a lake.

It was isolated by design; they had picked out the location for this very reason. In the summers, people used the area for haunted house challenges—there were some ruined buildings around that were rumored to contain ghosts.

In that sense, a headless woman riding a carriage made of physical shadow was certainly appropriate, but in fact, even that was out of place: Japanese ghost stories rarely had European-style carriages.

Celty and Shinra were worried about this at first, but they ultimately went with the location and embarked on a day-trip vacation.

The idea had been Celty's at first, to give Shinra a chance at some leisure time. He did so much for her on a regular basis that a vacation seemed like a good plan.

She fashioned herself a gothic black dress to match the carriage. In place of the helmet she normally wore, she had a ladies' hat with a matching cape. If they were pure white, it might have looked like an ornate wedding dress, but being made of shadow, they were more like mourning clothes.

But despite Celty's widow outfit, Shinra was perpetually hyped. At his request, she'd been "trying on" various shadow clothes all day, rather than just her typical riding suit. Given his utter devotion to her, no one could blame Shinra for being excited.

For his part, he wasn't wearing the usual doctor's coat, either. It was a special outfit he put together for the trip, albeit just as white-centric as ever.

His eyes sparkled brighter than ever before, and with every new outfit Celty changed into, he raised a cheer of delight.

In this case, "changing into" was more literal than usual: She was merely reshaping the shadow that covered her body.

♂♀

May 5, midday

"Say, Celty. About the changing, I have a request. If possible, I'd really like to see you remove your clothes each time so I can watch you wriggle your bare arms into the slee— *Buh!*"

She answered his request with an elbow. *"Pervert. What if someone saw me changing inside the carriage?"*

"Hey, if you've got the goods, show 'em off-aff-ahf-aaah!"

He did his best to smile through the pain of a twisted cheek. "Sorry, I was lying. I don't want anyone else to see you. Your changing scenes belong to no one but me-hee-haaa!"

The flick to his temple did far more damage than he was anticipating. Meanwhile, Celty had rearranged the shadow she was wearing into a new outfit.

"I'm all done."

Shinra read the words off the PDA being held in front of his face, then glanced over the device at Celty.

There she sat, looking somehow shy and embarrassed, in a girl's school uniform of all black.

"I brought the red scarf from home and tried wearing it, but it just made me look like a girl at one of those brothels, I think..."

The fact that she had no head made her more like the victim of a freakish school murder mystery than a prostitute, but Shinra did not mention this. He assumed a very serious look and folded his legs atop the carriage seat.

"What's wrong? Is it weird after all?" she asked, uncertain what this reaction meant. She was about to reform the shadow clothes to the usual riding suit when Shinra suddenly bowed his head, tearing up.

"I've loved you from the first moment I saw you. Will you go out with me?"

"That's really creepy, Shinra. What's gotten into you?"

Maybe that blow to the head earlier really did a number on him, she wondered, suddenly worried. Perhaps she ought to turn the carriage around and rush him to a hospital.

Shinra wiped his tears and grabbed her arm. "No, no, I'm sorry. See, I always wanted to make one of those high school declarations. I used to dream of how I would ask you out if we went to the same school..."

Celty shrugged and typed, *"You're a lot of trouble, you know that?"*

"Even when other girls asked me out, I had to tell them, 'You're nice and all, but you still have a head on your shoulders'..."

"Go track down those girls and beg forgiveness, right now. Also, is the insinuation here that you would take any woman without a head?" she shot back.

Shinra shook his head violently. "No, not at all! I would love you without reservation, Celty, whether you had a human head, or a cardboard head, or some amalgamation of slugs and earthworms!"

"That's disgusting!"

Actually, I'm kind of amazed that there were girls who liked this freak, Celty reflected. *You've gotta be a real eccentric...*

"But once the rumors got around, the girls got creeped out and stopped approaching me. In fact, Shizuo once unfairly complained to me that the girls were avoiding him, too, all because of me."

"That's not unfair at all."

"It isn't? Well...I guess you're right. Of course you are," Shinra said and laughed like a child.

Eccentric? she thought. *Well, I guess that does describe me. The eccentric who loves a woman without a head, and the eccentric who fell in love with him.*

Smirking inwardly, Celty typed away on the PDA's keyboard.

"Why are you so focused on clothes, anyway? Something tells me this is more of a male thing than you specifically."

"I don't know about other guys. All I know is my own reason. To me, you are unlimited possibilities. If I'd been born in a different time or place, I know we would have met all the same, just under different circumstances. And I want to experience all those possibilities!"

"I didn't realize it was such a grand vision."

"Oh, that's just my excuse. The truth is, I just want to see you in all different outfits so I can get all horn...," he said, stopping in the middle of his sentence and bracing himself.

"What happened? Can't you go on?"

"Oh, I j-just figured I'd get another elbow... Wait, I seem to recall another instance of this, a few months ago..."

Celty tried to remember. *That's right. Things were happening just like this, and then...I think that was when Emilia rang the doorbell and interrupted us. She just grabbed Shinra and hugged him. I could barely believe it.*

She could laugh it off now, but at the time, Celty had been on the verge of jealousy. She felt both ashamed of that behavior and secretly pleased at the reminder of how much she loved him.

Honestly, I wonder…why did I fall in love with him?

In her past, somewhere among the memories locked in her head, had she experienced a life like this one, as a proper fairy back in Ireland?

On a vacation with her lover: a very picturesque moment of bliss, according to a human being. Had she ever experienced bliss like this in her old life? What was her life like back then?

She couldn't deny being curious. But…

"What's wrong, Celty? Are you feeling bad?!"

"No…," she replied, looking at Shinra's face.

At this point in time, her present life was far more important than whatever was in her past. She decided to enter a teasing message into the PDA and placed it on Shinra's knees.

"And what were you going to do…after you got all horny?"

"Huh…? …!"

"If you get all horny here in this carriage, what's going to happen to me?"

"…"

Huh? He's not saying anything, she realized. Normally, he would act surprised at first, then burst into excitement. Instead, he merely stared down at the PDA in silence, his face neutral, if not downright serious.

Uh-oh… Did I tease him so much that he got mad?

She was going to snatch back the PDA to type out an apology when Shinra clutched her hand.

"Celty…"

He looked deadly serious, which was not his normal way. But the redness in his cheeks was kind of creepy.

"I, erm… Thanks."

Oh…

"Thank you…Celty."

He's thanking me?!

"I'll try my best!"

Your best at what?!

She really wanted to type these quick-fire responses out, but she still hadn't retrieved her PDA yet. If she was thinking calmly, she could have just stretched out her shadow to get it back, but Celty was nowhere near calm at the moment.

Every last facet of her being was radiating a general state of fluster.

He reached toward her shoulder, his eyes dazzling and sparkling.

No, w-wait...

When Shinra was fooling around like usual, she always socked him to get him to stop, but when he looked *this* serious, Celty was suddenly unsure of what she wanted to do.

At least let me cover the carriage windows! she pleaded silently, when—

♪ ♪♪♪   ♪♪♪♪   ♪ ♪♪♪♪ ♪♪

A ringtone went off in Shinra's pocket. It was the new song from Ruri Hijiribe, a singer whom both Celty and Shinra greatly admired.

Celty took advantage of the situation to snatch Shinra's phone and press it against his face.

"*Mrrlb!*" he protested, the cell phone jammed into his mouth. Celty finally got back her PDA and sent out a multitude of tiny finger shadows to type for her.

"*You've got a call, Shinra.*"

"Forget about it. Now's not the time."

"*Don't forget, you're a doctor. Legitimate or not, there are people's lives in the balance waiting for you.*"

"Well, if you insist...," he said, dejected, and answered the phone.

"Hello?"

Meanwhile, Celty took the opportunity to think.

Wow, that was a shocker. It's not like we've never done anything like that...but I wouldn't have expected it here. Plus, I feel a bit embarrassed knowing that Shooter's just nearby...

"Oh? Ohh, ohh! It *has* been a while! You're still alive—should I be congratulating you on that?"

Still alive...? He must be speaking to the Awakusu-kai, or someone along those lines.

"Goodness me, has someone shot you? You certainly sound well enough over the phone."

Yeah. I knew it.

"Uhh...I'm not going to ask about the circumstances. Is tomorrow night all right?"

Tomorrow night. So it's work—I guess we won't be spending the night around here.

"I'm afraid I'm off duty today. I'm not in Tokyo at the moment."

Well, that's all right. We'll plan out another occasion, maybe rent a cabin in the mountains.

"...She *was*?"

Wait...he's looking a bit paler now. What are they talking about?

"And I suppose the humane thing for me to do is stop you?"

No, really, what are they talking about?! Is it Mr. Shiki claiming he's going to bury a body or something?! Why confer with Shinra, then?!

"Well, in this case, that girl happens to be Celty's cooking teacher."

Why did my name come up?! Teacher? Cooking teacher?! Oh, d-does he mean...?

"Huh? They hung up."

"*What was that, Shinra?! Who was calling?! When you said 'teacher,' did you mean Mika?*"

♂♀

Shinra registered Celty's apparent consternation and thought hard.

What should I do? If I tell her what the call was about, I'm certain that Celty will immediately rush off to help her. That much is a guarantee. That's what makes her Celty. And I sure do love Celty!

While Shinra might have been satisfied with the bedrock status of his love, he was hesitant to be truthful here. The woman he had just talked to was the very person who ran off with Celty's actual head. It was quite possible that things might go strangely and end up putting the head back into Celty's hands.

And Yagiri did clearly say that her intent wasn't to kill.

So given all the factors at play, he made a quick decision and gave her a huge, guilt-free smile—and a total lie.

"It was Seiji Yagiri. He just got into a little fight of some kind. Nothing to worry about."

"Oh. I see."

"   "

...

"   "

...

Yes, Celty literally typed out the ellipses to emphasize her silence.

"........................."

The headless woman in the schoolgirl uniform held up her screen to his face, using her shadow tendrils to continue typing. Each additional ellipsis put more pressure on Shinra's conscience.

"...Ha-ha! Oh, Celty," he pleaded awkwardly, but she sent forth more shadows to hold him down.

"Don't lie to me! It's her! That had to be Namie Yagiri!"

"Ohhhh! You've learned to detect when I'm lying, just by looking into my eyes! I love that—it's like our hearts are more connected than ever!"

"You wouldn't say 'Has someone shot you?' or 'You're still alive' to Seiji Yagiri!"

"What a detective you are, Celty! Fine...I'll fess up," Shinra said, sighing. "Namie is planning to revert Mika's face to its original state. But Mika really enjoys that face, you know? So she wanted to know if I could do some surgery on her tomorrow, while she's sleeping. So the question was, is it humane?"

"I see."

"And I wouldn't want to get in trouble for something like that, would I? I mean, she's your cooking teacher. So when I brought that up, she got mad and hung up. The reason I lied is because I was afraid that if I brought up Namie's name, you might go after her to chase down your head..."

Celty withdrew the shadows that were holding Shinra's body down. *"You're such a fool, Shinra. How often do I remind you that I don't care about the head anymore?"*

"I know you say that, but I'm still scared. Maybe the head will manage to suck you toward it instead."

"You're overthinking this. Anyway, what is that woman up to? Does

she finally feel guilty about messing with that girl's face? It's ironic that Mika herself doesn't want her old face back."

As he read Celty's message, Shinra thought to himself, *I'm sorry, Celty. She just doesn't understand the dangers that Namie Yagiri poses... The call was actually way more menacing than I made it sound. I still just don't want you anywhere near Namie...and that head.*

By baldly lying at first, and then fessing up by telling what was *almost* the entire truth, Shinra ultimately succeeded at throwing Celty off the trail. It was less that he tricked her than that he simply omitted some crucial details, but at any rate, it successfully kept Celty away from Namie.

Well, after that...I guess we can't just pick back up where we left off... plus it feels like I just abandoned poor Mika. But hey, she said she wasn't going to kill her...

He glared down at his phone, blaming it for dousing the steamy situation with a bucket of cold water, and was about to turn it off when Celty showed him a new message.

"How about I change the mood by switching into my next outfit?"

Instantly, all thought of Mika Harima and Namie Yagiri was gone from his head.

"What? Already?!"

Of course, given that he had originally performed surgery on the girl's face in order to fool Celty, it was hard to see how abandoning Mika was any worse than what he'd already done.

"No, Celty, wait! I want to savor feeling like a student a little while longer! I want to look up to you as my upperclassman...but then, I also want to be the older student treated with reverence...," Shinra babbled.

Celty suddenly stopped, then used her shadows to hold down Shinra once again.

"Aaah! What's this?!"

"Sorry—hang on a bit."

She sent a message to her headless horse, Shooter, and brought the carriage to a stop at the side of the road. As Shinra watched with bewilderment, she exited the booth.

"Wait...where are you going, Celty?! Hang on! Don't abandon me! If I did something wrong, I'll fix it! If it's about last week's episode of *Mysterious Discoveries of the World* getting erased, I apologize!"

His plaintive cry vanished into the woods, which Celty walked through, still dressed in a school uniform.

Ten minutes later

After what felt like an eternity in the carriage alone, Shinra was overjoyed to see Celty return, as if nothing out of place had happened.

"Celty! You came back!"

"You always overexaggerate."

"But…but…I was really starting to think that you'd abandoned me once and for all."

"Don't be silly. I would never leave Shooter behind," she typed curtly, while undoing Shinra's shadow bonds. *"Actually, I felt something for the first time in a while, perhaps a fairy presence? So I went to give my acknowledgments."*

"Fairy?"

"In Japan, I guess you'd call it a yokai, or a god of the mountain, or something. Anyway, there's lots of stuff out in the forests here. It reminds me of the woods back home," she noted wistfully, but given that she had lost her head and most of her memories, that particular detail had to be very vague indeed.

Shinra chose to avoid poking that topic. Instead, he smiled and asked, "So, did you get to say hello?"

"Yes…well… There wasn't any outright hostility or anything. It just said, 'Welcome to Japan'…and then…"

She typed out her hesitation into the message, her shoulders hunching in apparent embarrassment. *"It said it hadn't seen one together with a human in quite some time, and…it wished me luck."*

"Well, we'll do it proud! What a nice spirit! But wait…does that mean it was watching us?"

"It said…the man was making so much noise, it couldn't not hear us…"

"…"

If she had a human face, it would be beet red. Combined with the school uniform, he thought, the restless fidgeting made Celty look just like a youthful student.

"Ha-ha-ha, in that case, let's show off and— *Gwufh!* Wh…why?!"

He had put his hand on her shoulder, earning him a jab to the throat.

"More importantly, Shinra…what was that about last week's show…?"

"Eep!" Shinra was tied down with shadow for a third time before he could make any excuses.

"I was saving that for later… I was hoping that we could try to guess who would win the top prize on the show!"

"Aaaaah! S-sorry, Celty, sorry! I'll make it up to you with something worth a gold prize from the show—no, crystal prize! It'll be worth it!"

"Dum-dummm! (foghorn sound) Instead, you get tickles!"

"N-no! Not when I'm tied down and helpless! I'm sorry, Celty! It's too much for me, but on the other hand, being tickled by you is a heavenly thought, but on the first hand, please no, please no, please yes!"

Ten fingers of shadow stretched forth, about to descend upon Shinra's helpless flank—when his phone abruptly rang again.

"…"

"You can answer it," she offered, picking up the phone with her shadow fingers and holding it to Shinra's ear. His expression was a mixture of relief and disappointment as he spoke.

"Hello…? Oh, hi, Shizuo."

Shizuo, huh? He had a rough time of it yesterday, too, Celty thought, recalling how her friend had thrown motorcycles, kicked cars like balls, and saved little girls. She chuckled secretly, a bit of mirth that tamped down the burst of annoyance she was feeling.

"No, no need to thank me. Actually, I've got my hands full at the moment—or should I say, I've got them tied down… Yeah. Yeah, no problem. We can do that tomorrow."

That was apparently the end of the call. Shinra sighed heavily and said, "I'm sorry, Celty… I'm sorry."

"Don't apologize now," she replied, all snarkiness gone. She freed Shinra and looked out the window of the carriage.

The lake in the middle of the forest reflected the sunlight, a brilliant gleam flickering through the trees. The presence she felt earlier had waned. There were no figures around them anymore, not even any animals.

The moment was beautiful, and the timing was right.

Then Shinra said, "I kind of wish you'd punished me a little," and she decided that she would tease him for his perversion.

"If that's what you want, that's what you'll get," she typed into the PDA and covered the carriage windows with shadow.

"Whoa, it's pitch-black!"

Heh-heh-heh, he's panicking.

"What's going to happen?! What will become of poor little me?!"

Now I'm going to sit back, do nothing, and watch him writhe.

"Actually, sitting in the dark with a girl wearing a black school uniform kinda gets me all warm and tingly inside!"

That's a good reminder that I was going to change outfits.

With the cover of total darkness, Celty felt at ease enough to undo her shadow outfit. It had taken considerable care to do it earlier without showing off too much skin, but in the darkness, she could afford to be more daring...

Just at the moment that her skin was most exposed, Shinra's cell phone went off, sitting on the front-side seat.

The phone screen lit up the interior of the closed space, pulling back the darkness—and giving Shinra a glimpse of the soft curves of Celty's body.

"Wha...?!"

Hyaaaa!

...

Hyaaaaaaaaaaaaaaaaaaaaaaaaaa?!

She panicked, instinctually covering Shinra's eyes, then her own body, with a layer of shadow. Shinra felt around blindly for his phone, picked it up, and then answered in a daze.

"Hello... Hello...? Ahh...it's you... Yeah, I know... Probably at Yagiri Pharmaceuticals, Warehouse Three... Your sister was saying something about luring her there or whatever... Yeah. So long," he said, his voice bleary and absent. Celty hadn't been taking the words in, though.

She was in a mild panic, far too preoccupied to pay attention. Once she had replaced her shadow clothes and desperately regained control, she finally opened the carriage windows to the world again.

When the soft light of the forest caught her properly, they showed that she was so hasty in dressing that she was now clad in pitch-black armor of the type she wore back in Ireland. It was very strange to see her with that look, holding a modern PDA—but Shinra did not even register the armor.

"*D-did you see that, Shinra?*"

"...Huh?"

"*I—I know you've seen that back home, but I'm not as comfortable with being seen in a place like this. Plus, as I said, Shooter's right there... I'm quite shy about it,*" she typed in little fits and bursts. Shinra merely smiled with beatific serenity.

"It's all right, Celty."

"*What's all right?*"

"You're so cute, Celty. Hee-hee."

"*Gross!*"

I broke him! I broke Shinra! she realized, as he laughed eerily to himself. She tried slapping him to bring him back to his senses.

"*Get a grip! You hear me? Get a grip!*"

"Bwuh! Bwap! ...Oh. Oh, Celty. Why are you wearing armor?"

"*Huh? Uh, er...because...*"

"Armor... I see. It's the dullahan's basic cultural garb. I had never considered this! It might downplay your femininity, but I can sense your cuteness oozing out of it!" raved the man. Celty had pulled him out of the realm of fantasy only for him to travel to yet another dimension.

But for her part, she didn't seem to mind the compliments. Given that it was her basic outfit in the distant past, this seemed to be an affirmation of what she'd always been. In fact, she was so embarrassed with delight that she started to change yet again.

"No! Wait, Celty! Let me take a picture!" Shinra pleaded, holding up his phone as her shadows began to writhe. At the instant that she changed into new clothes, with part of her arms and legs exposed—though not as badly as the previous instance—Shinra pushed the photo button with perfect timing.

Except that another call arrived at the same time, switching the phone out of camera mode.

"Aaaaaaaah!" Shinra shrieked in rage, nearly screaming. "Wh-who did that?!"

"Well, that's one of the more bracing ways I've ever heard a person say hello over the phone."

"Oh, it's Izaya. Good-bye."

"Hey, don't hang up. Listen, I'm bored, and I can't move right now. I finally got the chance to borrow the hospital phone."

"Hospital? You're in the hospital?"

"You didn't watch Daioh TV this morning, then. I got shanked yesterday."

"Oh, cool. Good-bye." Shinra abruptly hung up.

"...Who was that from?"

He blithely answered, "Izaya. Says he got stabbed and is in the hospital now."

"What? Is he all right?" she typed, alarmed—then reconsidered and replaced that message with: *"Well...whatever the details are, he probably earned it, right?"*

"Of course he did."

"And if he called you, he must be doing just fine."

"You bet. He sure sounded fine over the phone."

Realizing that neither she nor Shinra were at all concerned for him, Celty considered the topic of Izaya. *I guess he's just the type of person you don't worry about when he gets hurt...like Shizuo, but for a different reason...*

"Still, I think you might have been treating him a bit coldly right there."

"It's fine. Izaya's the kind of masochist who loves people even when they're mean to him."

"Oh, look who's talking. Still, you have to watch out for infections and blood clots with stab wounds. You should probably apologize later. I mean, Shizuo and Izaya are the only friends you have..."

"Yeah...I should. If you say I should."

Yet again, Shinra's cell phone went off.

"See? Speak of the devil. Izaya's probably feeling lonely and worried, after being stabbed like that."

"Fine... Hello?" he said into the phone. Celty watched him, smiling inwardly.

"Yes... Yes... Huh...? No, I'm a friend of Izaya's... Sorry, I'm on a vacation right now... Reason he would be hated? Geez...there are so many, I couldn't begin to narrow it down. He's been getting himself into trouble ever since high school. Me? No, I'm clean as a whistle."

Whatever conversation he was having, it was a little strange. He didn't seem to be talking to Izaya. And the phrase *clean as a whistle* gave Celty a little start.

Now that I think of it, I've hardly heard any idiomatic expressions or extravagant vocabulary words from him today. Usually, he likes to throw them around to display his intellect. Maybe...he's feeling nervous or forgetting to do it because he's enjoying the trip... I really hope it's the latter.

Just then, the call ended.

"Who was that?"

"...The police."

"Huh?"

"They wanted to know if I knew anything about Izaya getting stabbed. They probably just redialed the number from the hospital phone. Phew! I was terrified that they found out I was a black market doctor! Felt like I was dragged from my vacation dream right back into real life."

Shinra slumped his shoulders, and the phone went off yet again.

His cheek twitching, he answered the call—and heard Izaya's voice through the speaker.

"Yo. Did you just get a call from the cops?"

"Yeah, thanks a lot."

"I see. Well, it's been so boring here. You were bragging about being on holiday, so I got a little mad. Thought it would be funny if the cops called a black market doctor. How was it? Exciting? Did the extra thrills just rekindle things with Celty? I'm assuming she's there with you."

"Ha-ha-ha! I wish you'd rekindle your body and burn to death."

Shinra hung up and went back to being dejected.

Once again, the phone rang.

"If you don't knock it off, I'm going to tell everyone about that thing from middle school, Izaya!" Shinra snapped in a rare display of anger—but there was no response.

"...?"

He thought this was strange, until he realized that next to him, Celty was holding her own phone up to around where her head would be. He checked his screen.

Above the number was the contact name—CELTY, MY HONEY.

He looked from the phone to Celty, back to the phone, and then figured it out.

"Ha-ha!" he giggled, and then his face softened to a grin.

"Thank you, Celty. I really do love you."

The words she'd heard hundreds, thousands of times...

They came both from Shinra's mouth and from her phone.

Sandwiched between both sources of sound, she came to a sudden realization.

Oh. I get it.

This is happiness.

She took her hands away from the PDA keyboard and sat back to listen to Shinra talk. She allowed his voice into her mind, and he read her emotions to produce words. Sometimes, they just stared at each other.

It might have looked like Shinra was holding an entire conversation on his own, but in truth, he was deftly reading her emotions, giving the impression that they were having a two-way discussion.

Eventually, he closed his mouth, and they sat shoulder to shoulder for a while.

Oh. I see, Celty thought idly.

It was something so ordinary, so matter-of-fact, she hadn't felt it necessary to even think about before.

But, to Celty, just the recognition of this fact made the entire holiday meaningful.

I really do...love Shinra.

After this, they would run across an attempted murder in the mountains, get attacked by a bear that escaped from the zoo, and wind up in the crosshairs between two groups attempting to win a prize by finding the supposedly extinct Japanese wolf, among other events with a higher level of "extraordinary" than usual—but those are stories for another time.

For now, unaware of these future events, Celty and Shinra were enveloped in love.

The black carriage trundled along with its pair of lovebirds aboard—*chaka-poko, chaka-poko.*

And right on the beat in between those sounds, Shooter the shadow horse issued heavy snorts through the cracks of the helmet that was supposed to represent its head.

As though they were heavy sighs of exasperation over the two lovey-dovey dopes in the back.

Chaka-poko, chaka-poko, shuffa-huff, chaka-poko.

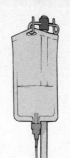

DRRR×7
Ryohgo Narita

Epilogue & Next Prologue Ordinary Fugue

Ikebukuro, in a car

"See, that doesn't just apply to series; it also holds true for voice actors. The act of putting down other actors just to prop up the actors you like isn't despicable for a voice actor fan—it's despicable for a human being."

"You can't avoid that. Those kids are too dumb to know how to applaud their favorite actors, so they have no choice but to put down others. You have to ignore them and give them pitying glances."

"I don't know, Karisawa. That sounded unnecessarily harsh to me…"

"The real question is, should it be Fan x Hater? Or Hater x Fan?"

"Oh, you're shipping them now? Wait, is this between two boys or two girls? The distinction is crucial."

Like any other day, Yumasaki and Karisawa were carrying on with their nerdy arguments as the van rolled on.

"It was so peaceful today," Kadota said, reclining in the front passenger seat, which was lowered all the way back. Sitting next to him, hands on the wheel, was Togusa.

"Isn't that a good thing?"

"Well, after all the crazy stuff that went on yesterday, I figured we were due for a follow-up…"

"But it's more usual for nothing to happen."

"Yeah, I get that…but think about the last year. We've seen a bunch of shit: Headless Rider, cursed swords…" Kadota grimaced. Togusa smiled, too.

"That'll change your outlook on life, for sure. I could believe in ghosts or aliens right now. Those are the second most-unbelievable experiences of my life after sitting first row at a Ruri Hijiribe concert."

"…Really? That was your number one? I wonder where Kaztano got those tickets," Kadota said, stretching and looking out the window at the town rolling past. "See, the thing about the world is it always finds a balance. While we're here relaxing and doing nothing—I'm not gonna bring up that hackneyed bit about orphans in some war-torn country across the globe—there's probably some other spot in Japan where things are all wild and out of control."

"What's your point?"

"We're involved in this Black Rider and Dollars stuff now." Kadota smirked, pulling his beanie on and adjusting the seat back to its upright position. "We just gotta be prepared for all that trouble to come find us."

♂♀

Tohoku region, hospital

"…Who are you?"

It was deep into the night, and the hospital was silent.

A woman with murder in her eyes was now at Izaya Orihara's bedside.

Clearly, she was not here to wish him well. In fact, the knife in her hand said she was more likely coming to finish him off.

There was just one problem: Izaya could not, for the life of him, recall who she was.

"Who…? Who am I…? Oh…of course. I suppose that I was never even worth remembering to you…"

"It must be true since I honestly can't remember you," he said. It sounded like a sardonic rebuttal, but it was a simple fact.

She didn't get angry. In fact, there was even a little smile on her lips when she leaped into action.

"And now, this person not worth remembering will be the very one who kills you."

She hurtled up onto the bed, landing with both knees.

"Gah!" Izaya gasped, the impact shuddering through his body and wrenching at his wound.

"Ha-ha... Serves you right. Now the tables are turned... You're the one who's immobile. I'm the one who lives."

"...?"

Now the tables are turned? What...what is she referring to...?

Something beyond the door of his memory was pulling at him, hard. But he couldn't recall what it was.

As he scrabbled at his memories, the woman held her knife right to his throat. "I won't make it simple... You don't believe there's an after-life, so you don't think there's any suffering afterward, do you? That means we have to get all your suffering in while you're alive, don't we?" She grinned, seeking agreement.

An ordinary man would tremble at her obvious madness. But Izaya was less afraid than he was stunned by what she had just said. The impact rippled the sea of memories, bringing fragments of the past up between the waves.

Why would she be mentioning the afterlife...?

No, wait...I remember talking about that.

Yes, I did...

That's right! It was a year ago...

The night I first met Mikado Ryuugamine!

"Are you going to try screaming for help? That would be great... I'll take you hostage—you'll look really pathetic on tomorrow's news. The man who fancies himself an information broker in Shinjuku, brought nearly to death by a mere woman—come see the emperor's new clothes! I'm sure that bartender you hate would be delighted to hear about it," she gloated.

Izaya buckled down, forgot the pain, and gave her a dazzling smile. "Actually, Shizu never even checks the news. He doesn't want to get annoyed by a stupid story and then destroy his TV."

Ignoring the screaming agony of his wound, he bolted upright, rolling off the hospital bed with the woman. His IV needle popped out, sending clear liquid flying through the darkness.

"Ah!" she gasped, trying to regain her position, but the gap in fighting experience was devastatingly clear. Izaya might have been the analytical type, but he'd been in plenty of deadly brawls with Shizuo Heiwajima and other ruffians.

Instantly, he was on top of the woman, wresting the knife away from her. He tossed it back and forth, playing with it, and grinned. "Seems like you took some lessons…but not enough of them, I'm afraid."

"…Kill me. Then you'll be a murderer. I don't know if there's an afterlife, but at the very least, I can spend my final moments imagining your miserable state as the police chase you down."

"Kill? Kill you? That's silly!" he mocked, shouting loud enough that his voice might have reached the next room over. "I would never bother to do that! I'm not charitable enough to kill a suicidal person for them!"

"…So you *do* remember."

Izaya Orihara had not actually recalled the woman's face or name. But he could remember exactly what she was.

Last spring, he had been dabbling with a particular type of game. He went online under the alias Nakura, luring people from pro-suicide websites into real-life meetings, then taking everything from them but their lives and observing the results—an extremely cruel, tasteless game.

This woman was one of the two suicidal victims whom he last met, on the night he finally got tired of the game. What did those women look like? How were they dressed? Were they beautiful or ugly, stylish or unfashionable? What did their voices sound like; why did they want to die; did they even want to die at all?

Izaya thought he had forgotten all of it. But what memories he did have were enough to tell him that she was one of those two women.

She was not worth remembering in the least.

But now she was here as an entirely different person.

And that knowledge, that truth, lit a fire to explosives that had been dormant deep in his heart.

"Ha-ha… Ha-ha-ha-ha-ha-ha! Ha-ha-ha-ha-ha-ha-ha-ha-ha-ha-ha-ha!"

He laughed, easily loud enough to be overheard. He laughed, and laughed, and laughed.

"Yes. Ahh, yes, yes! *Insignificant, unmemorable you!* But now, the half-hearted wannabe suicidal has embraced hatred of me, nurturing it over an entire year, found my location in less than a day based on the news, and came to find me!"

"...?"

She stared at him in suspicion, completely baffled.

"That's right! You came here! You came here! I don't know how you tracked me down, but could there be anything better?! You betrayed my expectations of you!"

Izaya got to his feet, dragging the woman up with him by the arm—and then embraced her, squeezing tight like reuniting with a lover after years of absence.

"Thanks to that...Thanks to that, I remembered! I've been able to return to my roots."

Yes, that's right. That's right. Perhaps, after obtaining that head...I was underestimating humanity. I assumed that there was something greater than humanity.

"But how about this? Look, me! Take notes, me! *Humanity is brilliant!*"

"..."

Had there ever been a lottery winner who celebrated this much? The woman felt a thrill of horror at this level of excitement from him—but her hatred was so strong that it won out.

"I don't know what you mean, but I can say one thing."

"What's that?"

"You're a disgusting excuse for a human being."

"That's fine," Izaya said, grinning from ear to ear like a child who'd just gotten the toy he always wanted. "No matter how much you hate me..."

"I love, love, *love* you—to an almost irrational extent."

Several minutes later, a nurse reported to Izaya's room after receiving word that there was noise going on in the middle of the night.

She found nothing there—no Izaya, no woman, no changes of clothes or belongings.

*   *   *

Where did Izaya Orihara go?

Those who knew Izaya would find out—but not for a little while yet.

♂♀

Near Kawagoe Highway, apartment building

"Boy, that was wild."

"I never would have expected that."

An exchange of text and words was happening inside an old elevator.

"Just when I thought we'd actually found an extinct Japanese wolf, it turned out to be a werewolf? It was just crazy. And those priestesses at the shrine were weird. They seemed kind of vampiric."

"It's the first time I've seen *one of those* aside from you and Saika, but you're still the best of them all!" Shinra raved.

They were reminiscing happily about the adventures of their vacation, exhausted. Once they'd started riding on Shooter—as a two-seat motorcycle again—they hadn't been able to talk, so now was the time they could finally discuss all the wild events of the day.

The elevator stopped rising, then opened. Celty put a cap on the discussion by saying, *"Let's start by taking a shower."*

"How about together for once?"

"Don't get ahead of yourself."

She knuckled Shinra's head and started walking down the hallway, her mood buoyant.

The usual schedule would return tomorrow. Today's memories would be the fuel that carried her through the day's courier work.

But before she could reflect any further than that, she heard a very unexpected voice.

"Good evening."

It came from up ahead.

From the mouth of a boy sitting in front of Shinra and Celty's apartment door.

"I thought you might not be back tonight. Another ten minutes, and I would've left."

The boy looked even younger than Mikado Ryuugamine. Celty recognized him at once.

It's him!

The boy who had offered Mikado a deal in that abandoned factory, just one day ago.

"Mikado wouldn't tell me anything about the Black Rider, so I had to get here on my own."

"Who are you?" Shinra asked.

The boy smiled softly and said, "Aoba Kuronuma. I've met the Black Rider on a few occasions."

"And I've come here...to be friends with you two."

...

Celty had years of experience observing humans.

The only people who spoke about becoming friends on a first meeting were either the blindingly innocent or the devious. The boy named Aoba Kuronuma was undoubtedly the latter.

The red color seeping into the bandage on his hand only made Celty feel more nervous. What if that "normal schedule" did not return to their lives after all?

Aoba mocked her anxiety, waving the bloodied hand in the wind. It waved and wavered, blown by the clammy breeze...

Quietly matching the anxiety and uncertainty saturating the city. Wave, wave, waver, wave.

A holiday does not exist to rest the body.

It is not for resting the mind.

It's not the body or the mind that relaxes…but the entire "state" of everyday repetition.

That is what I wrote at the beginning.

But there is something you must not forget.

On the morning that you tell yourself to drink deeply of the extraordinary on your holiday, so that you might return to the ordinary in a refreshed state—do not forget that the usual repetition may not return.

What did I tell you? The city does not distinguish between ordinary and extraordinary, work and rest.

It always comes down to people to see and judge these things.

Human beings.

So there's no guarantee that the new day the city provides for you after a holiday will be the same as what you had before.

There is always change and evolution within the typical day—but I do not speak of such small matters.

This would be akin to eating healthy every day, then enjoying the occasional steak on the weekend. Except that rather than returning to healthy food, you are suddenly served a full-course poison mushroom meal.

If you do not receive the ordinary life you expected and instead must swallow a bizarre set of circumstances you never wanted…

I suggest you pray.

And trust that your stomachs are at least as strong as the city's.

—Excerpt from the afterword of Shinichi Tsukumoya, author of Media Wax's Ikebukuro travel guide, *Ikebukuro Strikes Back 3*

CAST

Celty Sturluson
Shinra Kishitani

Izaya Orihara

Shizuo Heiwajima
Tom Tanaka

Mikado Ryuugamine
Anri Sonohara

Masaomi Kida
Saki Mikajima

Mika Harima
Seiji Yagiri
Namie Yagiri

Akane Awakusu
Kururi Orihara
Mairu Orihara

Walker Yumasaki
Erika Karisawa
Kyouhei Kadota

Shiki
Aozaki
Akabayashi
Mikiya Awakusu

Vorona
Simon Brezhnev

STAFF   ILLUSTRATIONS & TEXT DESIGN
        Suzuhito Yasuda (AWA Studio)

        BOOK DESIGN
        Yoshihiko Kamabe

        EDITING
        Sue Suzuki
        Atsushi Wada

        PUBLISHING
        ASCII Media Works

        DISTRIBUTION
        Kadokawa Publishing

AUTHOR   Ryohgo Narita

AFTERWORD

Hello, I'm Ryohgo Narita. It's been a while, hasn't it? Or if you're new, welcome. I hope you stick around!

Anyway, as those of you who bought this book around its release date probably already know...

THE *DURARARA!!* TV ANIME SERIES HAS BEGUN AIRING!

As of this writing, I've seen a few episodes already—and I can barely contain my excitement at their quality. In fact, I'm so excited I've got a fever of 101 degrees. Okay, that was a lie. I'm just sick. But I'm also so happy that I could get up and dance to express my delight!

But enough about me being silly. I'd like to provide a little afterword to each of the stories in this book.

RENDEZVOUS BOLERO

Namie and Mika are both top-class "broken" characters among the female cast of *Durarara!!*, but I feel like their relative lack of profile in the story allowed them to be passed off as normal for too long. Actually, I was considering a backstory where Namie took on a girl who was approaching her brother and seduced her to pull her away from Seiji...but it would have pushed the page limit, and I had moral concerns, so I didn't write it in. If you're a fan of the *yuri* women-who-love-women romances, please employ your imagination.

OUTCAST CONCERTO

This is a story of Akabayashi, my personal favorite. But as a matter of fact, I named most of the Awakusu-kai figures after editors at the Dengeki Bunko office, so my personal editor often says things like "I have a hard time imagining this guy being the hero of the story, because I always see Takabayashi's face on him." It's not fair! Anyway, there's also the mother of a character whom I won't reveal for fear of spoilers. It's a bit different from the usual *Durarara!!*

COLLECTION RHAPSODY

On the other hand, this one was very appropriate, in my opinion. Shizuo thinks of his ideal woman as an older lady, but in order to find out more about that, you'll have to wait for an original anime story in the near future (major announcement!). After this, I think Akane and Vorona will remain as regular cast members orbiting around Shizuo. The cast tends not to grow much in *Durarara!!*, so the introduction of new members is a valuable occurrence.

LOVEY-DOVEY *CHAKA-POKO*

In this story, the sound *chaka-poko* is used to represent the clopping of horse hooves, but I got the term itself from the famous novel *Dogra Magra*. That aside, I really wanted to put Celty into a school uniform. I considered adding a cheerleader outfit and elaborate kimono, but I doubted that anyone really cared that much aside from me and Shinra.

HOSPITALIZATION POLKA

At first, I planned for Izaya to have an extremely boring Golden Week with no visitors. But a certain character in the manga edition (I won't say whom) was drawn so incredibly cute that I had to put her back into the story... That led to quite an interesting development with Izaya. I wonder what will happen? Even the author doesn't know.

Speaking of the manga, the comic edition of *Durarara!!*, drawn by Akiyo Satorigi, is running monthly and just had its first volume released!

I'm very much enjoying *Durarara!!* in these new forms, drawn and animated from different points of view. I really hope that all of you out there enjoy this multimedia blitz as much as I do, if not more!

By the way, the first DVD of the anime series is already slated for release in February. Not only will I be writing a short story for it, but there will be other bonus goodies as well, so if you've got some money burning a hole in your pocket, I highly suggest checking it out!

On top of that, the *Baccano!* artbook by Katsumi Enami will also be coming out, so give that a peep, too! My days are overflowing with excitement and pride knowing that so many things are coming out related to my works. Thank you for all your support!

*The following is the usual list of acknowledgments.

To my editor, who has to put up with my constant nonsense at all times, Mr. Papio. To managing editor Suzuki and the rest of the editorial office.

To the proofreaders, whom I give a hard time by being so late with submissions. To all the designers involved with the production of the book. To all the people at Media Works involved in marketing, publishing, and sales.

To my family who do so much for me in so many ways, my friends, fellow authors, and illustrators.

To Director Omori and the rest of the anime staff, and Akiyo Satorigi and Editor Kuma for the manga adaptation.

To the anime writers, starting with the series writer Mr. Takagi, Ms. Ohta and her idea for Kaztano's background, Mr. Nemoto who depicted a part of Shizuo's backstory, and Mr. Murai and Ms. Yoshinaga whose ideas served to influence even my writing process.

To Suzuhito Yasuda, who took time out of his busy schedule to provide the thrilling and enticing front cover and interior illustrations, as well as some design work for the anime.

And to all the readers who checked out this book.

To all the above, the greatest of appreciation!

"Celebrating his temperature sinking under one hundred during the writing of this afterword"
Ryohgo Narita

"I'M NOT DOING ANYTHING. ALL THE DOLLARS DID THAT TOGETHER..."

The holiday isn't over yet. The day after Izaya was stabbed, the scars of the recent incident are still fresh in the city. An eccentric couple wanders the town together as a sister keeps an eye on the girl hanging around her brother. Two women—one a child, one an adult—pursue the meaning of strength, focusing their attention on the strongest man in town. A set of mischievous twins don't bother to care about their brother. A yakuza clings to his past. Meanwhile, an underground doctor just wants to enjoy a vacation with a recently relaxed headless dullahan... Ikebukuro is going to be busy!

US **$14.00** CAN $18.50

ISBN 978-0-316-43968-8

E A N

9 780316 439688

51400 >

AGES
13 & UP

Follow us on

or at yenpress.com

Cover art by Suzuhito Yasuda

Printed in the U.S.A.